THE
BRIDESMAID

A Romantic Suspense Story

ANNE TROWBRIDGE

THE BRIDESMAID

A Romantic Suspense Story

ANNE TROWBRIDGE

ISBN: 979-8-9865072-4-8

*For my mom, Sarah, who was always my role model
for the strong, smart, and independent woman
I wanted to be.*

*Thank you for always believing in me
(and for reading everything I write!).*

Other Books by Anne Trowbridge

The Curveball Incident Series

Curveball: A Love Story (Book 1)

Curveball: A Wedding Novella (Book 1.5)

Out of the Park: A Romance (Book 2)

Thrown: A Baseball Romance (Book 3)
(coming soon, but available now in Kindle Vella)

Ticket to Love Series

The Honeymoon: A Second-Chance Romance (Book 1)
(also available in Kindle Vella)

The Bridesmaid: An Insta-Love Romance (Book 2)
(also available in Kindle Vella)

Cruz Into Love Series

The Distance Between Us:
A Hidden-Identity Romance (Book 1)
(coming soon, but available now in Kindle Vella)

The Friendship Divide:
A Friends-to-Lovers Romance (Book 2)
(coming soon, but available now in Kindle Vella)

What Separates Us:
An Enemies-to-Lovers Romance (Book 3)
(coming soon, but available now in Kindle Vella)

Author's Note

This book is set in 2003, in the time following the 9/11 terrorist attacks in the United States. As a trigger warning, readers should know it contains mentions of terrorist acts, both real and fictitious.

Prologue

"OH, HONEY, you're gonna look gorgeous in that dress!" the seamstress said as she fluttered around. "You *sure* you don't want to try it on again?"

"Nah, I trust you," Julianna replied. She shoved the dress into the garment bag she'd just been conned into purchasing.

"You're going to wrinkle it!" the seamstress cried, nudging her out of the way with her hip. Then she took the dress back out and eased it into the bag instead, straightening and smoothing it as she went.

"What do I owe you?" Julianna asked, bracing herself.

"Hmm, let's see.... There's the dress itself of course, and the alterations. Plus the garment bag. And then there's the sales tax, of course. Let me get that total for you."

"Great," Julianna said with a sigh. *Stupid, ugly, overpriced dress* she grumbled to herself as she dug her wallet out of her purse and handed the woman her credit card.

"Thanks, hon!" the woman chirped.

Julianna signed the receipt, grabbed the awkward bag, and made her way out of the shop. At a price tag of more than double what she'd mentally set as her limit, and as painful as the expense was to her and her bank account, the final tally wasn't so bad compared to what she *could* be paying in a city boutique for a designer label. That's how she rationalized it to herself, anyway.

Back on the sidewalk, Julianna folded the bag in half so she could carry it more easily. As she struggled with it, a cab pulled up to deposit its passenger. She hadn't planned on taking a taxi, but since there was one right there, she also had no intention of ignoring fate's little gift.

It's about time something went my way today, she thought as the cab's passenger finished paying and got out. Julianna pitched the garment bag into the backseat and then crawled in after it.

"Port Authority," she called up to the driver as the polite ex-passenger closed the door behind her.

"Thanks," she said through the glass, finally glancing up to acknowledge the man. As the cab pulled away, she caught a glimpse of his curly hair and his bright blue eyes.

Chapter 1

Living in Other People's Love Stories

THE TAFFETA confection swirled over Julianna's head in a cloud of Barbie-pink as she groped around trying to find the armholes, her arms pinned awkwardly over her head.

"You'd think I'd be able to figure these stupid things out by now," she muttered, torn between ripping the dress off and struggling a while longer to fit into it. Knowing she had to succumb to it eventually, though, she sighed and gave in. With one final stretch, she found the left armhole, then was able to target the other. Relieved that no seams were popping, she tugged the dress past her head and smoothed it over her hips.

Turning around, she looked into the full-length mirror.

"Oh, give me a break! I look like Bridesmaid Barbie," she said. "This is so embarrassing."

The dress *was* completely wrong for her. The length, which hit her in the middle of her shins, did nothing to accentuate her almost-six-foot height. The very full skirt, topped with tulle, shot off her rounded hips, creating more of a shelf than the bell-shaped ballerina effect the bride had promised her. And the color was just, well, too "preschool ballerina" for a thirtysomething to pull off.

"If I was still eight and maybe four feet tall, this dress would be the one I'd pick," Julianna said.

Her sister laughed.

"Well Jules, it's not like you didn't know what you were getting into," Megan reminded her. "What is this, like, your tenth wedding?"

"Yeah, you're really helping. It's *only* my ninth," Julianna replied, laughing as she caught her sister's eye in the mirror. "I know, I know. I seem to be going for some sort of world record. I don't know why I can't get out of this cycle."

Except she did know why—and it didn't have anything to do with being a romantic sap who dreamed moodily about her own wedding while repeatedly conning her way into someone else's big day. She was quite happy with her life just the way it was. While other women, both during and after college, had been actively open to finding their life partners, she had been studying while cultivating friendships. She loved hanging out with the girls, shopping, going to the movies, hitting the flea markets, going out for after-work appetizers and frothy drinks.

But that was back when she was surrounded by all her single friends, laughing and dishing on the latest gossip. Now they all seemed to be paired with their mates, like they'd gotten a call from Noah and were headed for the boat. But she hadn't gotten the same call.

It wasn't that she had anything *against* dating or falling in love, really, but she just didn't ever seem to have the time these days. Between her full-time job at the hospital—a registered nurse, she worked three twelve-hour shifts a week—her time spent with girlfriends and family, and her voracious movie habits, her life was a perfectly happy and perfectly *full* place to be.

Yes, dating and love would be okay if they fell in

her lap and didn't take up too much of her time. But the wedding whirlwind she'd gotten sucked into had started souring her on the idea of weddings, not to mention the institution of marriage itself. It seemed the more she saw of the whole mess—friends morphing into bridezillas, fighting in-laws, outrageous expenses, goofy traditions, and ugly dresses—the more it all seemed like a waste of time. Why bother being in the spotlight of one of these ridiculous situations? She'd seen enough from the sidelines to last a lifetime.

It hadn't started out that way. In fact, wedding number one had been pretty great—standing up for a girlfriend who got married their junior year of college. That bride, bless her forever, had asked Julianna to wear any dress she wanted since she was the only attendant. As a poor college student, Julianna recycled the dress she'd worn to her high school graduation. It had fit, no minor feat considering the midnight pizza orders and diner runs, and the style hadn't gone noticeably "out."

So that wedding—a trip to the justice of the peace at the town hall with a few friends—ended up being painless and stress-free. No expenses for the maid of honor other than whatever she had spent putting together a scrapbook for the newlyweds. It had been perfect, from Julianna's point of view. Also no parties, no fittings, no forced trips to a hair stylist to find a perfect updo. Just friends and love and a certificate. And since the two of them were still married, she figured she wasn't the only one who thought so.

As a result, it hadn't even occurred to her to say no when another friend, this time from high school, announced he was also getting married. Julianna, although she didn't really know his bride that well, was still honored and happy when they asked her to be a bridesmaid. Friends, love, happiness...what could be better?

But that was when things started to slide downhill. She wasn't the only bridesmaid; in fact, she was one of *twelve*. And the dress choice wasn't exactly debated and voted on democratically. The woman had been a nightmare, picking out and insisting on a yellow dress that warred wildly with Julianna's blonde hair and pale complexion, giving her a waxy look and making her feel like a big, frumpy lemon the day of the wedding.

And after all the money she'd spent on that day—between the dress, shoes, accessories, hair, makeup, and present—the couple hadn't even managed to stay married for two years. What a waste.

It only got worse after that. The funny thing was, none of the weddings started out big and none of the brides started out evil. It was always the same—*No, no, really. I promise. We'll find a simple, cheap dress that looks great on all of you, and you'll be able to use it again. Trust me....*

Every single time, no matter the type of wedding, indoors or outdoors, formal or informal, that was always the promise. And every time, she ended up wrapped in ruffles and bows and tulle and fabric roses.

"Use the dress again—hah!" Julianna burst out, making both of them laugh. Megan surely knew exactly what she'd been thinking about. It was a well-covered topic between the two, and the subject of much debate. Just how *could* those dresses be put to good use? Blocking drafty doors was the winning entry so far, although tire traction in a snowstorm was a serious contender.

"I hate to say this, Meg, but I can't wait for this stupid wedding to be over with," Julianna confessed.

"And after this, I'm hanging up my bouquet. I'm just sick of all of it." She added an overly dramatic sigh.

"Oh poor baby!" Megan teased, flopping down on the bed. "So many friends who love her and want her in their weddings! Life is so *hard!*"

"Oh shut up, you know what I mean. I'm just in a rut, I guess. I've spent so much time being in my friends' lives. I think I forgot to live my own." She made one last futile attempt to flatten the tulle. "I need a vacation. When's the last time we went anywhere?"

"Hmmm...was it the family summer trip to Niagara Falls the year before you went to college?" Megan asked. "After that vacation, you always stayed home each summer working."

"Yeah, I think that was my last trip," Julianna said absentmindedly as she now struggled to get back out of the pink concoction. "Wow, that's *really* depressing."

"Then let's go somewhere!" Megan told her. "You've got time coming, and my semester will be over in May. Why don't we just pick a spot and price tickets before we change our minds or chicken out? Oooh, how about somewhere tropical? An island in the Caribbean maybe."

"Nah, you know I can't take vacations in the sun," Julianna replied, finally pulling free of the dress. "Ten minutes on the beach and my pasty white skin becomes radioactive. Oh, hey, what about Europe? London, maybe? I think I saw a commercial about an airfare sale."

"That's a great idea! Perhaps I'll take a lift to my flat and stop in the loo after riding in a lorry," Megan babbled with a horribly affected accent.

"Yeah, okay, calm down there, Princess. Might want to bring it down a notch."

"Fine, but can't you almost taste the scones and tea now?" Megan asked with a smile. Then she was off to her computer to check the prices.

Julianna draped the dress on a hanger, shoved it into her closet, and sighed yet again. One more wedding to suffer through, then she was cutting loose. It was definitely time for an adventure of her own.

Chapter 2

Stranger on a Bus

THE FLIGHT from New York was overnight. So Julianna's excitement eventually gave way to exhaustion, but not enough to sleep.

She gave up all hopes of resting—or of getting comfortable, for that matter—and succumbed to her mental review of the trip. Aside from the usual London sites, they were also planning to take a few bus tours, including one to Stonehenge and the historic city of Bath. Bath—the site of an ancient Roman bathhouse and the setting of a couple Jane Austen books—was a destination that Julianna was particularly excited about. They also planned to tour Leeds Castle and see another historic city, Canterbury, on a second tour.

She couldn't wait. But she also worried again that she wasn't allowing herself time for the relaxation she knew she desperately needed. Would their nonstop plans wear her out completely?

Brilliant planning, she thought with a laugh as she shrugged off the worry. She wanted to wring every possible drop of adventure out of this trip. Relaxation would just have to book its own vacation.

When the plane touched down a few hours later, she was wide awake and eager to tackle their getaway head on. All worries about the itinerary had abandoned her; she was ready for fun.

They retrieved their suitcases from the baggage claim and breezed through customs without any problems. After stopping to load up on local currency, they caught the Picadilly tube line into the city.

Their hotel, which was on the northern edge of Hyde Park, appeared to be simple but elegant. They checked in, then hauled their suitcases into the tiny, two-person elevator and headed up to their room, which turned out to be small but comfortable.

They unpacked and got settled, then spent time walking around Hyde Park admiring the beautiful lawns and gardens. It was early May, which meant it still wasn't peak season for tourists. But the weather was unusually warm and sunny nevertheless. People were sunbathing or walking along the paved paths while sidewalk vendors sold ice cream, paintings, and crafts. A group of college-age boys were playing rugby on the grass.

"I'm going to be the first tourist in London history to get a sunburn," Julianna said to her sister. "Can you believe this weather?"

Megan smiled. "Well, I'm sure we'll see the trademark rain and clouds eventually."

"Yeah, but I don't care. Let it rain. Let it pour everyday if it wants to."

"Oh sure, that sounds just great," Megan grumbled.

"Nothing could possibly spoil this trip for me," Julianna told her. *Nothing will spoil my mood—not lack of sleep and certainly not bad weather,* she thought stubbornly. *Nothing will prevent me from enjoying this trip.*

I won't let it.

*   *   *

The next morning ushered in another sunny day, which was perfect for the first of their day trips.

Armed with backpacks full of essentials like water

and granola bars, Julianna and Megan queued up to climb onto the bus when it pulled up. Despite all of their planning, they'd had trouble finding the hotel designated as the meeting spot and were consequently at the end of a long line of tourists.

The tour guide who greeted them was a woman in her mid-fifties who was trying hard to blend in with the nursing-home set. Her almost completely gray hair was pulled back severely in a bun, and she had the worst case of sensible shoes that Julianna had ever seen. Julianna handed their tickets to the guide with a smile, hoping that the woman wouldn't pull out a ruler and rap her knuckles for not moving fast enough down the aisle. They were the last two to board, and there weren't many seats left.

Megan took the first empty seat without hesitation, no doubt spurred into action by the sight of the cute guy sitting there. Julianna rolled her eyes, ignoring her sister's wink, as she continued down the aisle. A woman was standing there who had to be in her late seventies or possibly early eighties, sporting blue hair and a bright red sweatshirt that had "Viva Las Vegas" splashed across it in glitter. She was in the process of claiming the last pair of open seats when Julianna spied her.

She ought to be fun, Julianna thought, heading in that direction. But as she edged toward the back of the bus, she heard a voice—a *male* voice—that she thought was talking to her. Shaking off the Vegas-grandma zone she was in, she stopped, then turned right to find its source.

What met her gaze was a sight she couldn't believe she'd missed in her original scan of the passengers—a pair of beautiful blue eyes that bore into hers. They were behind small, silver-rimmed wire frames, and beneath a blue Yankees hat. Short, black hair peeked from under the brim, and then she was back to those eyes. She could die happily just staring into them. They belonged to a guy—an American, if the sports affiliation was any indication—who looked to be in his mid-thirties. Dressed in worn jeans and a faded Springsteen concert shirt, he was every bit the tourist as she was herself, in her jeans and "I Love NY" sweatshirt.

With a start, Julianna realized the tour guide was urging everyone to get seated, while she was still standing there with her jaw hanging open. Plus, she'd never replied to whatever this Adonis had said to her. Smooooth.

"Are you okay?" Adonis asked slowly, as if he was trying to tame a rabid dog while simultaneously signing the words in American Sign Language.

"Huh? No, sorry. I'm just an idiot," Julianna said with a laugh. "Can I sit here?"

"That's what I offered you about fifteen minutes ago," he teased, patting the chair simultaneously.

"How do you know sign language?" Julianna asked as she sat down, stowing her backpack under the seat in front of her.

"I went to elementary school with a girl who was deaf. Mrs. Cassidy had us all learn enough to be able to talk to her. And you?"

"I'm a nurse. I took it in college, thinking it would be useful if I ever needed to treat a deaf patient. It's already come in handy a few times, so, y'know, I'm really glad I, um...sorry, I'm babbling." She stopped herself then and extended a hand to shake. "My name is Julianna Wright, and I live in New Jersey. My sister Megan and I are here on vacation. Oh, and look at that—I'm still babbling."

Adonis, straightening in his seat and taking her hand in his, laughed. "I'm Nat Grady. I live in New York, and you're welcome to babble all the way to Bath if you like."

Still unable to stop gazing in his eyes like a lovestruck teenager, Julianna was quite literally shocked by the electric tingling that shot up her arm and lodged somewhere suspiciously close to her heart. Nat looked a little startled himself, as though he'd felt the same thing.

"And on the way back to London?" she managed to say in a throaty whisper before a blush started burning her cheeks.

"Yeah, I think the offer will still be on the table," Nat said, a sexy smirk creasing his face as he added, "especially if you keep blushing like that."

Julianna nodded but found herself unable to say more in that moment, still shocked by her body's response to this man. She hadn't seen him standing, of course, but as she continued to stare dreamily at him, she would guess Nat was at least six feet tall and he had a lean, physically fit look to him. Add in the tanned face, and she presumed he spent a lot of time outdoors. "What do you do?" she finally managed to ask after realizing her gaze—and her hand—had never left his.

"I don't remember," Nat said, leaning closer until their foreheads met lightly. "I can't believe I'm about to say this, but I *do* know I want to kiss you. This is crazy, but is it okay, Jersey girl?"

She found herself unable to speak yet again.

Chapter 3

A Kiss From a Stranger

WHAT IS HAPPENING right now? she wondered as she continued to be absorbed by Nat's eyes and the swirl of electric emotion she saw in them. He hesitated then, his head tilting to one side as he awaited her reply.

Did she want to kiss a stranger? *Should* she? Was this whole thing completely crazy and irrational? *Yes,* she thought—and yet she found herself nodding the same.

"What's a bus trip to Bath without a kiss from a stranger?" she finally asked with a nervous smile, astonishing herself even as the words fell from her lips. But hadn't she just decided to start living *her* life *her* way? How better to achieve that than to dive headfirst into whatever *this* was....

"Oh, we're not strangers," Nat said as the bus pulled out from the station. "At least we won't be for long," he added, his voice husky and low before he silenced both of them with the very kiss he promised, at first sweet and inviting, but growing from warm to steamy in the span of a heartbeat. If Julianna's heart was, in fact, still beating—the electricity passing to her from this man was enough to defibrillate it.

"Wow," she whispered after pulling her lips back from his. Their hands were still lightly clasped together, and their faces remained close enough for her to feel his warm breath. "If you had been in the guidebook, I wouldn't have waited for the off-season prices."

"You're cute when you babble," he said, closing the small space between them to kiss her again.

"Sadly, you've never seen me *not* babbling," Julianna said before leaning in for one more. She didn't want to stop to analyze how crazy the last few minutes had been. She had never felt anything like this, and it didn't matter that the feelings flooding through her were completely unfamiliar.

As she pulled back to look into his eyes again, she said, "Okay, so, you haven't told me anything about yourself." She thought perhaps if she knew him better, these feelings—and these kisses—wouldn't seem so crazy after all.

"What would the cute babbling nurse from Jersey like to know?" he asked.

"Mmmm, well, are you here alone?"

"Not anymore," he said, smiling at her.

That beautiful smile was both her undoing and somehow the spell breaker. "Stop, you're killing me," she said. She noted nervously that Megan was gaping at her from her own seat further up the aisle. "If we don't slow down, they're going to throw us off the bus, then I'll never get to see Stonehenge."

"Yeah, you're right," he agreed, pulling off his hat to reveal a head full of beautiful black curls. He ran his fingers through them, then put the hat back on. "I'm sorry, Jersey. I don't usually attack women within five minutes of meeting them on the bus to Bath. You just seem to have that effect on me."

"Ahh, yes. I've heard that old story before," Julianna replied as she reached for her backpack, hoping some cold water would put out the fire that was currently burning inside her. "I've never acted this way before, either."

Or felt this way before, she thought again as she took a long sip, then turned back to Nat to offer him some. He nodded, reaching for the bottle. She watched him tilt his head back, his sexy, clean-shaven neck pulsing as he drank.

Nope. The water wasn't the answer to her problem. *Talking. Get him talking....*

"So, you never answered my question about what you do. What are you hiding, Mr. Grady?"

"Nothing. It's just not quite as interesting as saving people's lives like you do," he said. "I guess you could say I'm a student of human behavior."

"Like a psychologist?"

"Kind of like that, yeah," Nat said, reaching out to touch her long, straight hair.

"Great. Since I've met you, I've acted completely certifiable," Julianna said nervously, afraid his touch would make her leap back in his arms like a sex-crazed lunatic.

"I won't report you," Nat assured her, now twirling a strand of hair mindlessly as his gaze bore into her green eyes. "I'm sorry. I just can't seem to stop touching you."

"Me either," Julianna agreed. "I...okay, this really sounds like a line, but, like I said, I've never acted this way—or *felt* this way—before in my life."

"Pretty much what I was going to say," Nat said. "And before you ask, no I'm not married—not currently and not ever. I've *never* walked down the aisle, and I'm not seeing anyone right now."

"Oh really? I've walked down the aisle nine times," she said, trying to look serious, but failing miserably as Nat's eyes got noticeably wider. "Okay I was trying to see if you'd fall for that, but I'm a terrible liar," she said with a laugh. "I'm like a professional bridesmaid these days. Have ugly dress, will travel."

"Ahh, okay," Nat replied, clearly relieved. "You had me scared for a minute there."

"No, I don't get married, I just witness everyone *else* doing it. And I'm not seeing anyone, either. No time, what with my rigorous taffeta-buying schedule." She was now tracing patterns in his left palm.

"So I suppose you've got your whole wedding planned down to the mega-important white cake versus chocolate details?"

"No, I don't!" she said, and it came out a little too sharply. "I mean, you know, I used to. Like every junior high girl, I knew I wanted to get married, in what style dress, and all the other details...."

"Okay, then what happened?" Nat asked.

"Well, weddings two through nine happened," she told him, amazed that he seemed entranced by her every word. "Each one got more ridiculous than the last. Everyone's always fighting. And they're *soooo* expensive—especially in New Jersey, where weddings are a major industry—and they just become such a show. Somehow they stopped being about love and commitment and started being about oppressed bridesmaids, meddling relatives, huge price tags, and stupid traditions. So I just hate them now. I'm not having one."

"You're going to elope to Vegas?" he said, with an oddly quizzical look on his face.

"Won't need to. I'm never getting married."

"Oh," Nat said, looking a little...was that *disappointment* she saw in his face? Why would he care if she ever got married, or even if she shaved her head and moved to Tibet for that matter? *Is he thinking long-*

term?! she wondered, struggling to find the right response to his mysterious reaction.

"Is that 'Oh, that's just one more really fascinating thing I've learned about you in the last half hour'?" Julianna asked, still trying to decipher his crestfallen expression. "Or was it 'Oh, wow what a weirdo'?"

Nat laughed, dropping her hair and sitting back in his chair for the first time. "It's 'Oh, I'm disappointed,' I guess. I admit it, I'm a hopeless romantic. I guess I want everyone else to be one, too. I want one of those big, frothy weddings. And yes, complete with tortured bridesmaids. I want a house with a fenced-in backyard so our dogs and our children can run in circles while my beloved wife and I laugh, play, and make more children."

"And what does that sappy little dream have to do with me?" Julianna asked, a wicked smirk—and a telltale blush—on her face.

"You tell me, Jersey," Nat said, grabbing both her hands in his own. She noticed for the first time that they were fairly rough and callused.

What kind of psychologist has hands like this? she wondered idly as she looked down at them. Then she took a deep breath before answering him.

"I feel a strong pull to you, Nat. I really do. And this is crazy, but it's so strong and intense that I just can't believe it. And I can barely keep my hands off you. But it hasn't completely made me forget everything I know and believe to be true about myself and my life, either."

"Fair enough," Nat said, exhaling as though he'd been holding his breath. "Thank you for being honest. I'm sorry. Only a jerk would push you on such a serious topic so soon in the relationship."

"Relationship, huh?" Julianna said. She was smiling again.

"Yes," he said, a look of intensity radiating from those beautiful eyes now. "And I hope you're open to it, even if you've seen a hundred of your closest friends have a thousand crappy relationships."

"Yeah, I think I can find a way to deal with it," she said with a teasing smirk. Then she settled back in her seat, her smile stretching wider now as his declaration looped in her head.

I think I'm going to like Bath, she told herself.

Chapter 4

A Shot of Chemistry

"SO WHERE TO after this?" Nat asked. He obviously wasn't enthralled with the tour guide's story about the early Romans settling in Bath after being drawn by the natural hot springs. Neither was Julianna, for that matter.

"Stonehenge. Didn't you read the flier?" Julianna said, turning to peek at Nat. They were more than an hour and a half into their drive, and she was disappointed they were almost to their first stop, afraid it would break the spell that had woven itself between them.

"Very funny, Jersey nurse," Nat said, squeezing her hand, which he still held tightly in his. "Is this wit part of your bedside manner?"

"Nah, but it *is* part of my one-woman comedy routine."

"You're killing me. What I meant is what are you doing tomorrow? How long are you in London?"

"Oh that! We're here for two weeks, so we're doing lots of stuff. I made a detailed itinerary that involved spreadsheets because I'm super cool like that." She reached down and plucked it out of a side pocket on the backpack. "Hmmm...well, tomorrow is the British Museum in the morning, tea at Harrods in the afternoon, and a play in the evening. Wednesday we're going to the Tower of London in the morning, then shopping in Notting Hill in the afternoon. Oh, and this'll be fun—another bus trip on Saturday, this time to Leeds Castle and Canterbury."

"Did you schedule any time to breathe and go to the bathroom?"

"Are you accusing me of over scheduling?" she asked, raising her eyebrows.

"No, it just sounds a little, uh....*overplanned* to me," Nat replied. "What if you don't feel like shopping on Wednesday or sipping tea tomorrow afternoon?"

"Spontaneity has its time and place," Julianna replied, pointing to a line in the itinerary marked *Thursday: free day.* "See, it's right here."

"Okay," he said, shaking his head. "You planned your free time. You win, you're totally spontaneous."

"We just didn't want to miss anything. This is my first trip to Europe, and my first vacation in a looong time, and...."

"And what?" Nat prompted.

"And, well, you know. The first time I've done anything just for me in about as long as I can remember."

He smiled at her, and she saw that he understood. It was evident on his face. But something else was there, too. Was it a look of concern?

"Well, I hope you two are being careful," he finally said, a frown darkening his face.

"Yes, of course," she said a little defensively, hoping he wasn't about to reveal any caveman macho "women shouldn't travel unescorted" tendencies. "Trust me, we heard all about it from everyone we know, our parents included."

"Parents—they're still together?" Nat asked, a look of surprise crossing his face.

"Yes, it does happen occasionally, you know."

"Of course it does. But I figured your hatred of marriage might have something to do with your parents and maybe a messy divorce. I guess not."

"Nice psychoanalysis, Dr. Freud, but nope, just the opposite really. They're still completely in love after forty years of total bliss. I just don't think I'm destined to be that lucky. I think the bliss gene skips a generation."

"If that's the case, then I'm due for some serious bliss," Nat told her. "My parents' marriage was a train wreck. Luckily they put it—and me—out of its misery by the time I was ten. Thank heavens that nightmare ended."

"Then how did they raise such a sap?" she asked, smiling again.

"Well," he said, looking serious, as though her joking question actually held significance and weight. "Partly because it made me realize how I didn't want to end up."

"And the other part?"

"The Jersey Nurse Bliss Gene Theory, of course," he said with a wink.

"Oh, but of course!" she laughed. "I'm so glad you understand."

The rolling green countryside they'd been traveling through had now been replaced by a panoramic view of quaint city streets lined with stone buildings.

"Oh no, we're here," she said.

"That's probably not the slogan they're going with on the tourism brochures," Nat said. "What's wrong?"

"I just don't want...." she started before rethinking her words. "Nah, now I'm being the sap."

"You don't want this to end," he finished for her, his tone matching the tender look on his face.

"Yes," she admitted. "That's exactly how I feel."

"I don't want it to end, either," Nat said. "I'm intrigued by you. But just because we're in Bath doesn't mean it's over."

"I know, I know. This has been wonderful, Nat. Maybe one of the best days in my life, I think."

"Same here," Nat said, leaning down. "And I think we should acknowledge that with another kiss."

"If you insist," Julianna sighed happily, feeling the same burst of electricity as their lips met once again. "Bath is the best city I've never seen."

"Gonna babble again, huh?" Nat teased.

"You know it," she said happily, completely immersed in the sensations coursing through her body and oblivious to everything else.

And then the first shot rang out.

Chapter 5

Lots of Time

JULIANNA'S STARTLED scream barely escaped her lips before Nat was pushing her toward the floor of the bus and covering her body with his.

"Wha..what's going on?" she asked, but there was so much screaming and crying that she didn't think Nat heard her. "Nat? What's happening?"

"I think some gunmen decided to pay us a visit," he replied quietly, his face pressed against her back.

"Megan!" Julianna said frantically, now trying to push against the tight hold he had on her. "Nat, I have to see if she's okay!"

"Shhh! Jersey, please just stay here. I know you're worried, but really, you can't do anything right now. For what it's worth, I honestly don't think they shot anyone—just the roof of the bus."

"Who? Who's doing this? Where did they come from?" She was trying to keep her frantic questions to a whisper.

"Well," Nat whispered. "I haven't been officially briefed on the situation yet, but it looks like a couple of the passengers had guns."

She tried to force herself to calm down, but she couldn't stop shaking. The concern for her sister was threatening to overwhelm her as another shot rang out and the bus lurched to a stop.

More screams filled the air.

"Nat! Let me up! I have to go see if Megan's okay.

Please!" her voice cracked at the end, as her tears started to hit the bus floor, mixing with dirt and...*is that a potato chip?* she thought crazily, her mind too muddled to process her thoughts rationally.

"Please don't cry sweetheart," Nat said. "I'm sure Megan's fine. But I'm sorry—the bus driver's not doing as well."

"What? They shot him? Then who's driving?" she asked as the bus started rolling once again.

"One of the gunmen is driving. Listen, if I sit up, will you promise to stay down?"

Nat's words were just a small part of the deafening sensory assault she was under. The sounds swirled around her in a terrifying blur of screams, pleas, gasps, yells, and traffic noise.

"Wh..What?"

"I said if I sit up, will you please just keep your head down?"

"No! I have to go help the driver—I'm a nurse, Nat," she said, fighting to gain control over her emotions. "I have to go help him!"

"You can't help anyone if you charge up there like Wonder Woman and they shoot you, too. So just forget it. Let's wait and see where they're taking us first. Okay?"

"Okay, okay. I don't have a death wish. But I *will* help him as soon as I can," she said, looking up at Nat through tear-filled eyes as he finally released his grip on her.

She crawled up onto the seat again, trying to keep her head low.

"Here, lay your head in my lap," Nat offered.

"And what about your head? I don't want you to be a target any more than you want me to be."

"I think I can handle it," Nat told her, leaning into the joke until he saw the stricken look on her face. "Hey, no, seriously, I won't get shot, I promise. I'll sit low in the seat."

"You better," Julianna said before giving in and resting her head in his lap. During any other moment in her life, she would have been thrilled about being curled up in the lap of this funny, sweet, gorgeous guy. *But, of course, it had to happen at this stupid moment*, she thought, her mind still a whirling jumble of unprocessed confusion.

The bus kept moving, although Julianna lost track of time and distance as it seemed to wind aimlessly left and right.

"Are we even still in Bath?" she asked after a few minutes of eerie silence.

"I guess so, although the neighborhood's gotten sort of seedy. Well, as seedy as anything around here *can* look. It appears to be a warehouse district. Aaaaand....okay, now we seem to be stopping in front of one of them." He waited another beat before adding, "Yes, they're opening the door. Looks like this was their destination."

The bus paused for just a moment, then rolled closer to the door of one of the dark warehouses.

"Hey, Jersey, in case I don't get a chance to tell you this first...."

"Nat, please, you're scaring me," she said, tears starting to pool on his jeans leg. "We'll have lots of time to say it, right?"

"Yeah, yeah. We will. I'm sorry," he said, sighing as he ran his hand lightly over her hair. "Lots of time."

Chapter 6

Not Even Noon Yet

THE GUNMAN who had been driving the bus spoke for the first time.

"Get up! Leave your bags! Let's go, let's go!"

Julianna looked forward, straining for a glimpse of her sister. The other passengers started to move off the bus row-by-row, tears and shock marking their faces. The tour guide had gotten off first and, in an admirable attempt to soothe the others, was standing by the entrance of the warehouse greeting them like they'd reached a planned stop.

"Is that her?" Nat asked as Megan and the cute guy sitting next to her stood up.

"Yes, thank God," Julianna breathed as Megan turned her way, obviously looking for her. Their eyes met, and a look of relief passed over both their faces. Then Megan turned to walk down the aisle and off the bus.

"She'll be okay. She's with Tom," Nat said.

"Huh? You know him?" Julianna asked, confused. "I thought you were traveling alone?"

"I am, sort of. I work with him."

"Oh, that's great. And just how do you know that having a fellow psychologist with my sister is going to help keep her safe?" Julianna was snapping now as the terror for her sister clouded her thoughts. "Do you guys run bus-terrorist drills in your office?"

"Not exactly. Listen, that's part of what I wanted

to tell you. I'm not...oh, it's our turn." As they both stood and entered the aisle, he stepped in front of her. "Let me go first...."

Yep, he's at least six feet, maybe taller, Julianna told herself as she took a step back to let Nat by, before mentally chiding herself. *This is what I'm thinking about right now?*

They walked slowly toward the front, uneasy as passengers gasped when they went by the unmoving body of the driver before heading down the stairs of the bus.

As they approached the front and she caught a glimpse of the driver's limp figure, Julianna's instincts kicked in and took over her rational thought. As Nat turned to start descending the stairs, she tugged her hand free of his and reached for the first-aid kit attached to the roof of the bus above the windshield.

"Julianna, don't!" Nat barked, grabbing for her arm.

"Keep moving!" one of the gunmen, a middle-aged and surprisingly nondescript man, said from his spot nearby. His darkish hair and lifeless eyes couldn't be pinned on any particular nationality. Add in the souvenir London t-shirt, and Julianna could see how the guy was able to blend easily into the crowd of tourists.

When Nat didn't heed his warning, the man knocked Julianna to the side, bringing the butt of his rifle down on Nat's shoulder and kicking him in the chest.

"Nat!" Julianna screamed as another gunman—who was shorter and stockier than the first—standing outside the bus grabbed him and punched him in the stomach, bringing him to the ground. After the exchange, the man reached under Nat's shirt and took away a gun. Nat had a gun? Why would a psychologist carry a gun on a vacation? For the moment, though, Julianna didn't care, as long as he didn't get hurt because of it—because of *her*.

"I'm sorry! It's my fault, just don't hurt him!" she cried, turning back to Gunman One, who was still on the bus. "I just wanted to help the driver! I'm a nurse!"

"Okay, she stays," he answered with a shrug. "The rest of you keep moving!"

Julianna looked down at Nat, who was still on his knees. Clearly unamused at finding a passenger with a weapon, Gunman Two kicked Nat in the kidneys. As Nat fell forward, the man then stepped on his back and aimed the gun at his head.

"Please let him go! Please!" Julianna begged. "He didn't do anything except try to protect me! I'll do anything—just let him go!"

"No!" Nat said. "Julianna, stop!"

"You'd give your life for this man?" Gunman One asked her, ignoring Nat. "He's your husband?"

"Yes...No. I...I'm sorry. I can't think while he's still got a gun to his head. Please just let him get up," she said, tears falling freely down her cheeks.

"Okay, he'll let your man go. But I'm done making deals with you," he said, before adding something Julianna didn't understand to Gunman Two, who then took his foot off Nat and pulled him to his feet.

Nat turned to look at her, his eyes filled with an emotion she couldn't identify. Probably hatred or possibly disgust, she thought miserably, since it was her fault they'd been singled out.

I'm sorry she mouthed to him, crying harder now as Gunman Two started to tug on Nat's shirt, pushing him toward the door where the other hostages had gone.

Nat turned and walked away, but as he disappeared from her sight, he raised his right hand subtly behind his back, his index, thumb, and pinkie fingers extended into a familiar bit of sign language meant for her eyes.

I love you.

He...he just told me he loves me.

Impossible! *I almost got him killed!* she thought wildly. *And he hasn't known me long enough to say something like that!*

No way. It was absolutely impossible. Maybe he was just letting her know he's a Texas Longhorns fan. Yeah, it probably had nothing to do with sign language.

Still...she shook her head, unable to make sense of what just happened. Tucking the memory away to be thoroughly analyzed later, she sighed and turned to face Gunman One.

"May I please get the first-aid kit and try to treat this man?" she asked, thankful her tears were drying up for now.

"Do what you must," he said gruffly, turning his attention back to the other passengers, who continued filing past them.

She reached for the kit, then knelt over the driver. He was still breathing!

The blood had soaked his shirt, making it impossible to see exactly where he'd been hit. Julianna ripped open his shirt, sending buttons flying. The bullet had missed his chest, mercifully. It appeared to have hit his shoulder. She rolled him toward her, feeling under his arm. The pool of blood and exit wound in the back confirmed what she had hoped: The bullet had passed cleanly through and wasn't lodged inside.

Glad that she'd put on multiple layers that morning, Julianna yanked her sweatshirt over her head—it'd do nicely as a bandage—and dug around in the kit for the supplies she'd need. In her professional opinion, it looked like the bus driver would live as long as he didn't lose too much blood.

She sat up, straightening her sore back with a groan. This was no doubt the most amazingly strange day of her life—and it wasn't even noon yet.

Chapter 7

Waiting and Wondering

"JULIANNA!"

Megan's voice cried out from somewhere within the dimly lit room as Julianna waited for her eyes to adjust.

After she had finished doing what she could for the driver—which was little more than disinfect his wound and try to stop the bleeding with her tightly knotted sweatshirt—Gunman One had yanked her off the bus and marched her to where the others had gone. The doorway led to a long, dark hallway. When they reached the end, he shoved her through the last door, slamming it and sliding the bolt behind her.

"Jules! Are you hurt?" Megan asked as she ran up to her.

"No, no I'm fine," Julianna replied, glancing down at a shirt that was now soaked with blood. "All of this doesn't belong to me. I tried to help the bus driver."

"Thank goodness!" Megan said, crying as they hugged each other tightly. "I was so worried."

"So was I," Julianna told her. "I was frantic on the bus when I heard the first shot, and I didn't know if you were okay."

"Yeah, I'm fine. Come on and sit down," Megan said. "There's someone I'd like you to meet."

She pulled Julianna toward one corner of the cavernous room. The other passengers had broken into various groups, and most were sitting on the cold, concrete floor, leaning against the walls. A single bare bulb hung from the ceiling. Nothing was on the walls except peeling paint, and there were no windows.

"First I've got to talk to Nat," Julianna said, looking around for the familiar Yankees cap. "Where is he?"

"The guy you were gettin' busy with on the bus? I haven't seen him yet."

"No! He's got to be in here," Julianna said, her voice rising to a shriek. She pulled from Megan's grasp and whirled around to survey the room. "Nat? Nat?"

"Jules, I'm telling you, he's not here. Come on and sit down before those jerks come back just to shut you up."

She tugged Julianna over to where she'd been sitting by the cute guy.

"Jules, I want you to meet Tom Campbell. Tom works for the CIA. Tom, this is my big sister Julianna. She's a nurse."

Tom was probably a little shorter than Nat and had spiky blondish hair with a purposely haphazard style Julianna had thought only a Hollywood stylist—or possibly a wind tunnel—could produce.

Julianna didn't even feel the shake as her hand met the one Tom cheerfully extended. She stared at him in confusion, then spoke to Megan as though he weren't in the room. "Where did you say he works?"

"CIA. He's on a cool secret mission," Megan replied, dropping her voice to a conspiratorial whisper.

"No, no, he's teasing you," Julianna said to her sister before acknowledging Tom directly for the first time. "Nat said you two work together."

"You mean Agent Nathaniel Grady?" Tom asked. "Yes, we work together."

No wonder he had a gun. Duh....

"Wow this day really took a turn," Julianna said, sinking to her knees on the floor. "Why didn't he tell me?"

"Well, we're not exactly supposed to take out billboards," Tom explained. "This *is* a covert mission we're on. But when the bullets started flying, I felt I owed your sister an explanation and some reassurance. I'm not surprised Agent Grady didn't do the same with you; he's probably smart to play it by the book."

"No, I think he tried to tell me," Julianna said. He *was* going to tell her something, but she'd stupidly thought he was about to declare his feelings for her or something equally romantic to match the cover story she'd so easily believed. How naïve could she be? She—who'd teased Nat about being a sap—had cut him off as he was trying to tell her that the whole morning had been nothing more to him than a special-op coverup. Her cheeks burned with embarrassment.

"Jules, what's wrong?"

"I'm an idiot. Tom, where do you think Nat, uh, Agent Grady is now?"

"Well, he might have overpowered one of the gunmen and gotten away," Tom guessed. "I've only seen two of them, so that's not completely out of the question."

"Or...?" Julianna prompted.

"Or, well, more likely they're interrogating him," he said, looking startled when the color drained out of Julianna's face. "But he's trained to take care of himself in these situations. We both are."

"They found a gun on him and took it away," Julianna said before a flicker of hope lit her face. "Oh, do you have one too? You can get us out of here!"

"Well...no, probably not. Think about it. What am I supposed to do? Threaten to start shooting hostages unless they release us?" Tom's tone was still oddly chipper despite the sarcastic words and their precarious situation.

"Not funny. So why are two CIA agents lurking around tourists on a daytrip to Bath and Stonehenge?" Julianna shot back, irrationally ready to kill Cute Guy Campbell. "Or wait, are there more of you? Are you working with the Vegas grandma?"

"We'd received some intelligence that we were following up on. Turns out it was pretty solid information, and Grady's gut was right again," Tom said, ignoring her sarcasm and looking particularly smug about this.

"I'm glad you're so pleased about it," Julianna snapped. "But we're a little scared right now, and that's just not comforting."

"Hey, it's going to be okay," Tom said to Julianna while giving one of Megan's hands a reassuring squeeze. We're not here in a vacuum—the United States government knows exactly where we are. There's gonna be cavalry riding in. We just have to sit back and wait for it."

"I'd feel better if we knew what happened to Nat," Julianna said, leaning back against the wall and closing her eyes.

Megan scooted closer to her and leaned her head on her sister's shoulder.

"You fell for him, huh?" Megan whispered after several minutes passed in silence.

"Pretty hard, actually," Julianna replied, mad with herself for allowing tears to gather in her eyes again.

"Yeah, I kinda thought so. You looked so happy

and engrossed with him on the bus. I sorta like cute Agent Tom myself. What a cool job!"

"Where does he live?" Julianna asked, trying to shake off her self-pity.

"I guess they're based out of Manhattan. Part of some special terrorist task force put together after 9/11."

"Yeah, Nat did say he lives in New York. I never thought to ask him if that's where he's from *originally*, though. What about Tom?"

"Illinois, although I forget which town."

"Do you really think you'll see him again?" Julianna asked.

"Oh yeah. We already exchanged numbers. So who knows?"

Megan was three years younger, but Julianna always felt she was smarter by a few million IQ points. She and Nat hadn't exchanged even the most rudimentary pieces of information. She was lucky she thought to get his name. Then again, that might be exactly how he wanted it. You don't go through CIA training without knowing how to get information you want out of someone you're questioning. Especially an idiot like her.

"Hey, Tom?" Julianna asked.

"Yeah?"

"Why weren't you and Nat sitting together? And why were you both chatting up tourists? Shouldn't you have been focused on scouting for bad guys?"

Tom grinned. "That was part of Grady's plan. He told me to try to blend in with the tourists in case something like this happened. He also said we should try to find someone—like maybe a single woman—to sit with and make the cover look natural."

"Oh. Thanks," she said, leaning back against the wall again, her heart breaking. *So, I was a pawn.* Or a decoy. Or whatever the lingo was.

"Hey Jules, if I marry Tom, will you be my maid of honor?" Megan whispered.

Julianna whipped her head around to glare at her, then saw she was merely being teased.

"I'm thinking orange polka dots."

Julianna made a face in reply, then settled back against the wall again.

So much for her grand adventure.

Chapter 8

Finally Talking

"I'M FREEZING to death," Julianna said. The large concrete room was quickly turning into a walk-in fridge as the afternoon turned into night, and she'd kill for her sweatshirt about now. Nat had just been wearing a t-shirt, too. She idly hoped he wasn't also freezing, wherever he was. Then she decided it might serve him right.

"So am I," Megan told her. "And I still have my sweatshirt on."

Julianna then added hunger to the list. At least there was a bathroom, which they—along with their fellow hostages—had taken turns using throughout the afternoon.

"I wonder if they're ever going to feed us?" Megan asked.

At that moment, the sound of the deadbolt sliding open caught everyone's attention, silencing all other conversation in the room.

Gunman One, the terrorist who had allowed her to help the driver, stood holding his rifle as he scanned the room.

The moment he found Julianna, he barked, "Nurse! Come here!"

"Oh no!" Megan said, grabbing her arm.

"Megan, I'm sure they just want me to check on the driver. I'll be okay." She hugged Megan briefly, then stood up and headed for the door. "Maybe I'll even be able to convince them to let us have some food and blankets," she added over her shoulder.

Gunman One grabbed her arm and yanked her out of the room. He paused to ram the lock back into place, then shoved her down the hall. He stopped her again a few doors down, rather than lead her to the bus as she'd expected. Then he drew back another deadbolt and pushed her into the new room, which was much smaller than the one they'd just left, and he closed the door behind her.

So much for my self-appointed role as spokeswoman and chief negotiator for the hostages, she thought.

The lock clicked shut, but she barely heard it when she realized she wasn't alone in the small room.

"Nat!"

His crumpled form lay in the corner of the otherwise empty space. She ran over and knelt beside him.

"Hey, beautiful," he said, looking up.

"Hey yourself, Super Spy," she replied softly, startled by the puffy bruises that now covered his face and arms. "What happened to you?"

"I'm okay. It's no big deal. So, I see you've been talking to Agent Campbell," Nat said, sitting up. "Jersey, I'm so sorry. I tried to tell you; I really did."

"I know, I know. You were just doing your job," she told him with a self-mocking laugh. "Let's not talk about it, okay? I can only take so much in one day."

"It wasn't an act," he said, this time sounding a little annoyed.

"Yeah, whatever you say, James Bond. I'm a big girl. I understand. Just tell me what's going on."

"Yeah, okay," Nat said, looking a little frustrated with her for reasons she didn't really want to think about. "Well, you know I can only tell you so much, right?"

"Yes, yes. Or you'll have to kill me. I get it—I watch a lot of movies. Now tell me what you can."

With a deep exhale, Nat took off the baseball hat and ran his fingers through his curls, an act Julianna was beginning to recognize as his "I'm thinking" mode. It was kinda cute, she thought idly, before mentally kicking herself for getting sucked in again.

"We got intelligence that London—*tourists* in London, that is—were going to be a target of activity this week. I had a gut feeling that we shouldn't bother with a lot of the usual terrorist hotspots like planes, trains, and hotels."

"Too obvious?"

"Yes, there's that. But also because buses are one of the last modes of mass public transportation that don't involve security checks and X-rays of luggage and carry-ons."

"Subways and trains too, though," Julianna pointed out.

"Yeah, those too. But…I don't know. I guess my thinking was that those are more about where the commuters are, not necessarily just the tourists."

"And your information said just tourists."

"Yeah. Well, there was more to what we were hearing than just that, but without getting into specifics, I guess all you really need to know is that my gut told me we had to focus on the buses, and the right people trusted me to follow up on it."

"And two guys armed with concert t-shirts is the best the CIA could come up with to thwart the plan?"

"This isn't the only bus with agents on it. My gut's not *that* accurate," Nat said, reaching for her hand. But she swatted it away, anxious to hear more.

"Okay, so you follow your instincts," she said. "They believe you enough to send a bunch of teams out, and you guys sort of randomly stake out some buses. Now what? Is this what you thought would happen?"

"No, the intelligence we intercepted wasn't very specific. So we didn't know what we were looking for, really—suicide bombers, chemical leaks, other kinds of bombs...it just wasn't clear."

"Okay, okay. I get it, thanks. I'm scared enough—I don't need the whole list. So now something happened, and they took us all hostage. What good's it doing me to have Agents Nat and Tom here?"

"We were supposed to check in at various times in the day," Nat went on. "We've already missed several of those, so believe me when I say something's being done."

"Do you have a tracker on you?" she asked, a gleam of hope in her eyes.

"You *do* watch a lot of movies, don't you?" he said with a laugh. "Trust me, we have our ways. That's all I can really say right now."

She sat back against the wall and closed her eyes again, trying to absorb all he'd just told her.

"And Jersey?" he asked, disturbing the silence that had grown comfortably between them.

"Yeah, Super Spy?"

"None of what happened between us was planned, scripted, or faked, you know."

"Please don't," she said. "You can just let it go with a clear conscience now. No need to explain or try to make me feel better."

"I'm not doing that!" he snapped, raising his voice

at her for the first time. "Why are you being so stubborn?"

"Because it was too good to be true, and now I know why—it *wasn't* true!"

They glared at each other until he finally broke the standoff, shaking his head, closing his eyes, and rubbing his temples.

"Why did they bring me in here to you?" she wondered aloud, hoping to change the subject.

"Oh, I...um...was acting more injured than I am, hoping they'd go get you for me. Guess it worked."

"Well, you're quite the actor. Where's the Oscar nominating committee when you need it?"

"Fine. You're right. I'm an accomplished actor. I don't even work for the CIA. I just travel the world trying to pick up women in increasingly convoluted scenarios to practice my acting skills. In fact, none of this is really happening. We're on a Hollywood sound stage, and I think your travel agent owes you a big apology."

"Okay, I get it!" she snapped. "I'm sorry!"

The silence that ensued was no longer companionable. It had been replaced with tension and misunderstanding and unspoken apologies.

Then Nat said, "When they took me off the bus, didn't you get my signal?"

"Yeah. You're a Longhorns fan, huh?"

Nat just shook his head and chuckled.

Chapter 9

More Talking

IT WAS NIGHT now, and the rapidly falling temperatures were a bitter confirmation of what their watches were telling them.

"Come here," Nat said, gently pulling Julianna over to his side. "We're both going to freeze to death if we don't pool our body heat."

For once she didn't argue and just allowed her head to rest on his chest.

"Listen," Nat started, his voice still gentle. "I know that we barely know each other, and there's no real reason you should believe me. But I felt something today. Please tell me whether you felt it, too. If you didn't, I'll leave you alone. I promise."

Several moments passed without her answering. Nat sat patiently and quietly, holding her and letting her sort out what she wanted to say.

"You know I felt it, too," Julianna finally replied, her voice barely a whisper. "I'm just having a hard time trusting feelings that I'd never experienced prior to a few short hours ago. And frankly, I'm not sure whether I should trust you, either."

"Yeah, fair enough," Nat said gently, his lips moving quietly against the top of her head. "But I meant what I said in the bus."

"The part where you let me believe you're a psychologist?"

"Again with the comedy act. No, the part where I

said I want to have a relationship with you. I knew right away when you sat down, and I still feel it...even though you tried to get me killed."

"Oh, yeah. I meant to tell you how sorry I am for that." Julianna pulled away from her cozy spot on his chest to look him in the eye. "I don't know what came over me—I saw a wounded man and my natural instinct to help kicked in."

"I knew that; I'm just teasing you. I would have handled that differently if I'd really thought the situation called for me to get away. But I couldn't risk your life or the other passengers' lives. It definitely showed me what an incredible nurse you must be, though."

"But I would have died, too, if my stupid attempt at heroics had gotten you seriously hurt or killed," she said. "I'm really, truly sorry."

"Well, please just try to trust me. Until we get out of this situation, let me take the lead, and no more saving the world on your own, okay?" He reached for a piece of her hair and let it twist in his fingers.

"Yeah, I'll try," she agreed, settling back into her spot in his arms. "I'm so glad we're together right now."

"Me too."

Time crept by slowly as they sat, both of them lost in their own thoughts. Finally, stiff muscles got the better of Julianna.

"I'm getting sore sitting here," she told him, leaning away from him and stretching.

"Let's try laying down. Eventually we're going to need to get some sleep," Nat said. He stretched out on the cold floor and tucked his left arm under his head for a makeshift pillow, inviting Julianna to lay her head on his other arm. She did, snuggling in tight against him once more.

"Nat?"

"Hmm?"

"Where are you from? Originally, I mean. You were raised in New York?"

"No, Oklahoma City, born and bred," he answered proudly, then added more quietly, "So you might be able to guess why I chose the career I'm in."

"Oh, the bombing of the Murrah Building, of course. Wow, I remember all the news coverage. So it really changed your life, huh?"

"It's not like I lost any close family or friends," Nat said, "but you couldn't help feeling the shock and the anger. I never wanted to feel that helpless again. I wasn't doing anything important with my life at the time. I had gotten my degree in political science at OU, and I'd just sort of been banging around for a while, sitting in cubicles but not sure what I wanted to do with the next forty or so years."

"But after the terrorist attack you knew? Right away?"

"Yeah, I knew that day," he said. "I was at work that morning. We felt the ground shake, so we turned on the radio and eventually a television, and no one could believe it. People were bleeding and crying, trying desperately to call friends and family. And in the middle of all that chaos, I was just sitting there, totally shocked by how strong that feeling was—the feeling of knowing exactly what I wanted to do after that."

"Then what happened?"

"I filled out the applications, went through all the background checks and physicals and testing, then moved to Washington and started training at The Farm.

It was incredibly hard, and yet so amazingly easy at the same time. I just *knew* I was supposed to be there."

Julianna shook her head. "My story's so much duller than that. I didn't have any epiphanies. I wanted to be a nurse for as long as I can remember. So I just became one. Period."

"Trust me, you saved yourself a lot of wasted time and heartache. So where are *you* from?"

"Paramus, New Jersey," she said. "Home of shopping malls and deadly highways."

"Sounds beautiful," he teased.

"Oh yeah. What other city in the world offers three Macys in a five-mile radius?" she said with a laugh.

"Hmm, impressive."

The talk trailed off as the excitement of the day caught up with them both.

Julianna's intuitions were still telling her to be cautious. Nat lied once; he could certainly be lying to her still. But her heart didn't seem to care that they'd gotten off to a strange and rocky start. And it didn't care that their situation was precarious at best and that their lives were at risk.

How can I be in such danger, yet feel so secure? she wondered to herself as she drifted off to sleep.

Chapter 10

Vanished

SHE AWOKE with a start, completely confused.

"Wait, where am...?" Her question trailed off as her mind rapidly recalled the details of the previous day. *The bus. The gunshots. The blood. Nat!*

She sat up and spun around.

"I'm right here, beautiful," Nat said. "Take it easy." He was standing with his head to the metal door, listening intently.

"Wow, I can't believe they let us be alone together all night," Julianna said sleepily as she stretched. "Especially since they're obviously suspicious of your gun-toting self."

"I don't know. None of this makes a lot of sense. Unless they got spooked and abandoned us."

"Oh yeah, great."

"Shh," Nat said quietly, still focused on his listening.

"Did you hear something?"

"Yes, something's going down," he whispered, a look of intense concentration darkening his face. "I think our stay here at the Bath Hilton is about over."

A rapping at the door made her jump. Nat calmly knocked back.

They have a secret knock? she wondered silently. *Where's his decoder ring?*

The door opened, and a man she'd never seen before was standing there with a rifle in his hands.

"What's the status?" Nat asked him.

"So far, nothing. We've swept most of the building, and there's no activity that we've found."

"There were two of them that I saw," Nat reported.

"Let's keep going," the other man said. "We haven't found Campbell yet."

"Julianna, you stay here, okay?" Nat asked, his eyes pleading.

"Fine," she said, not wanting to do anything rash again that might get them killed. "But please be careful!"

"I always am," he assured her with one of his beautiful smiles before he and the other man disappeared, pulling the door closed behind them.

She stood up and rubbed her hands over her arms, trying vainly to warm up and to stop worrying about Nat and her sister. But as the minutes ticked by, she got sick of doing nothing. She tried standing at the door, attempting to listen the way Nat had, but she couldn't hear a thing.

Suddenly the door burst open, causing her to jump back in surprise. *Apparently surveillance skills aren't one of my untapped resources*, she thought.

A young British policeman—*or don't they call them "bobbies"?* she asked herself—was standing there, the other bus passengers filing behind him down the hall.

"Jules!"

Megan flew past the officer and into her sister's arms.

"I am *so* glad to see you!" Megan nearly screamed. "What happened? Have you been in here alone the whole time? Where's Nat?"

"Okay, Megan, give me a break already!" Julianna

said. "One question at a time!"

"Let's go," the policeman said, urging them into the flow of the others.

They walked out into the bright sun, everyone squinting to make the adjustment.

"They took me to Nat, thinking he was seriously hurt," Julianna explained to her sister as they joined the crowd of ex-hostages in a confused huddle. "He wasn't, though. So we just spent the evening talking, and I'm fine."

"Yeah, we sat in that stupid room after you left," Megan said. "We never even saw the gunmen again. This morning, some guy opened the door, told us we were free to go, and that's the end of the story. What in the world do you think happened?"

"I don't know. They got scared off by something?" Julianna suggested. "Let's ask Nat and Tom."

"Where *are* Nat and Tom?"

The two surveyed the crowd, confused and worried, but didn't see either of them.

"When did Tom disappear—wasn't he with you in the room?" Julianna asked.

"Yeah, he was right behind me."

"Maybe they're inside still searching, or they found a phone and are calling their headquarters or something," Julianna said, though these possibilities didn't help calm the surging feelings of panic that were rising inside her.

"Isn't someone going to question us or debrief us or something?" Megan asked.

Julianna looked around. "Like who?" There were no authorities anywhere to be seen. Even the young policeman seemed to have vanished. "Okay, come on, this is too weird. What's happening?"

"Where are the police?" Megan asked. "Have we just been abandoned here?"

Julianna could feel the crowd starting to panic as similar worries and frantic questions filled the air. The tour guide tried to regain some control over the situation by saying that everything would be fine. Despite a night spent on a concrete floor, the woman in question looked impeccable, with not one hair on her head out of place. Her collected appearance and calming manner seemed to back up her authority, and the group gathered more closely around her.

At that moment, a bus turned the corner and headed toward them. It was identical to the one they were on the day before, obviously from the same company.

It pulled to a stop, and the door opened.

The tour guide greeted the driver by name. Apparently that was enough of an assurance; with a shrug, the first man in line headed for the door, stopping to offer his hand to help his wife up the stairs. The other passengers followed their lead and started filing on board.

Julianna couldn't do it. She wanted some answers first. Leaving her sister's side, she ran back to the door they'd just exited and yanked on the knob.

It was locked now.

She pounded it with her fists, then kicked it a few times for good measure.

"Nat? Nat? *Nat!* Where are you?" she called, the volume increasing with each word. Her effort was met with silence.

"Come on, Miss, let's go," the bus driver called.

"Jules, come on!" Megan added. "Let's just get out of here! They obviously had to go report in or something. I'm sure they'll find us later!"

With a sigh, Julianna gave in. She walked over and followed her sister onboard. She couldn't help noticing there were no bullet holes or bloodstains. *Must really be a different bus*, she thought. Megan sat down in the same area she'd sat in the day before.

"I'm going to try to get my own seat toward the back and lie down," Julianna told her, pulled by an invisible force to the same general location where she'd met Nat.

Miserable, she plopped down and then slid over to the window seat in a pathetic attempt to feel closer to him. She leaned her head against the glass and closed her eyes, letting her suppressed tears fall at last.

As she battled with her emotions, she hoped she could just fall asleep and forget this nightmare. That's when she saw it, sitting right where she'd left it the day before.

Her backpack.

Chapter 11

Staying

THE NEW BUS DRIVER stopped at a gas station on the way out of town for a bathroom break and food stop. Afterward, Julianna sat with her sister, the two munching on the granola bars from their backpacks.

"What do you think it means?" Megan asked, wondering how their belongings came to be there.

"It's got to be the same bus," Julianna said. "It's got to be. But when was it repaired? And who did it? Also, where did our trusty CIA duo disappear to and why? And what happened to those gunmen?"

"Why take us hostage and then leave us there?" Megan added, tossing the wrapper from one bar into her pack and ripping open a second.

"Hmm. I don't know," Julianna said. She absentmindedly reached for her water bottle, then blushed as her mind fell back to when Nat was drinking out of it yesterday. He made the act of drinking water blisteringly sexy.

She sighed and shook her head. Thoughts like that weren't going to get her the answers they wanted. They weren't doing much to help calm her frazzled emotions, either.

"Let's just talk out the possibilities," Megan said. "Maybe we'll come up with some sort of logical explanation."

"Yes, of course. The Wright sisters and logic: Your

two-step guide to figuring out the global terrorism threat."

"You're a scream. Really," Megan said, elbowing her sister for good measure. "No, I just think all of this means something, and even a couple of amateurs like us could figure it out if we try."

"Well, I wouldn't want to be accused of suppressing your inner private investigator, but honestly, Meg, all I truly care about is where Nat is and whether he's safe."

"Are you kidding me? You get held against your will and a man is shot, and all you care about is some guy you just met?"

"Am I shallow if I say, 'Yeah'?" Julianna asked, a teasing smirk on her face.

"Yes," Megan snapped, obviously not ready to find the humor in the situation. "You know I can't stand it when things don't make sense. Please just help me think this through before I go nuts. You can fixate on your new crush later."

"Oh, all right," Julianna finally agreed, although at that point she just wanted to avoid a fight. "Okay, well, let's start with the bus. Why fix it up so quickly?"

"Hmm. I guess just so no one else knows what happened," Megan suggested.

"But here we are, a busload of people who can easily run to our embassies or call the media and tell everyone everything."

"Do any of us have a shred of evidence though?"

"Not with the bus repaired and sanitized, and the injured driver missing, no," Julianna said. "I have my bloody shirt, but I'm not exactly thrilled about the idea of marching into a local police office and declaring that I witnessed a shooting. And since we don't have any other proof, we'd just spend our vacation being questioned with no good outcome."

"Right, so at best we look like a bunch of loonies," Megan reasoned. "And even if, say, a reporter or two believes us, how far will the story really go?"

"Yeah, not very far," Julianna agreed.

"Okay, so now we're onto something," Megan said, squinting as she concentrated, her mind whirring almost audibly. "Let's assume it was, in fact, our cute CIA team and their other squad members who figured this out, saved the hostages, and made the whole thing go away so it doesn't make the news. Now what?"

"Well, aside from the fact that they saved a whole busload of people, they've also succeeded in not giving the terrorists a spotlight," Julianna pointed out.

"Yes, that's true. But so what? It seems like there are terrorist activities reported every other day. Why hush this particular event, especially since it didn't turn out so terribly?"

Julianna shrugged. "Yeah, I don't know. Hey, unless they had information or evidence—or whatever—that this was just a signal!"

"A signal? You mean to alert other terrorists that it's time for something even bigger?"

"Sure. So now nothing else will happen because no one's going to hear about it!" Julianna said smugly, momentarily pleased with their brilliant spy work. "Good work, Lois! Do you think we should call Clark and Jimmy?"

Megan rolled her eyes, then turned to look out the window. She fixed her gaze on a flock of sheep dotting a hill, lost in her own thoughts for a while.

"Or maybe this *is* just a precursor to a bigger event," Megan started, "and the CIA's going after those bigger fish. Maybe they covered this up to *let* the other one happen. You know—so tourists wouldn't freak out and go home, or so local authorities wouldn't scare the terrorists into hiding."

"That idea in itself is pretty scary," Julianna commented.

"Do you think we should go home?" Megan asked.

"Well, if we're right that no one heard about this, then Mom and Dad and everyone at home shouldn't be freaking out about us," Julianna replied. "And so far, all we've gotten is a really thorough examination of the highway system between London and Bath. We never even got to see Stonehenge."

"Yeah, I know. This whole vacation sucks so far."

"Well, I can't say I regret it, only because I got to meet Nat, even if he totally disappeared on me. And I really don't want to just chicken out and go home. Otherwise, I'm letting everyone else dictate my life again." She turned to her sister then, her eyes pleading. "Come on, we have to at least stay and see a few things, don't you think?"

"Yeah, I suppose we knew all about terrorism when we got on the plane," Megan said. "I guess it would be stupid to let it scare us right back home. And what are the odds of us stumbling into something twice?"

"Hopefully not high."

"Yeah," Megan said with a shrug. "So I'm game if you are."

"Thanks, Meg!" Julianna squealed, giving her baby sister a big hug.

"Yeah, don't think I don't know that this has a lot more to do with seeing a certain cute guy again than with any burning need to tour Buckingham Palace."

"Oh shut up!" Julianna replied happily, reaching for another granola bar.

With the bar set this low, the trip has *to get better,* she thought.

In that moment, she was absolutely sure of it.

Chapter 12

Back at the Hotel

THE BUS PULLED UP in front of the tour's headquarters at Victoria Station, and a man in a suit came toward them. Julianna figured he must be the owner or manager.

As the weary, disgruntled, and disheveled passengers started getting off, the suited man greeted them, apologizing and handing out free tickets for another day trip. Julianna and Megan wearily accepted theirs as they got off, stepping aside to discuss what to do next. None of the other passengers seemed to be making much of a fuss, either. *Wasn't the tour company's fault*, Julianna thought.

"What do you think?" Megan asked. "Should we bother going to the embassy or the police?"

"Honestly, I just want to go back to the hotel and go to sleep," Julianna admitted. "I feel like our government knows perfectly well what happened to us. Why bother?"

"Yeah, good point. Okay, let's find a cyber café first, though. Even if Mom and Dad didn't hear about what happened, they're gonna wonder how we're doing."

"Do we tell them?"

"Nah. Why worry them? Besides, if they knew, they'd call everyone from the president to the local animal control, freaking out and demanding someone do something."

Julianna nodded. "Yeah, you're so right. We should probably just skip over a few details. Let's go."

They put on their backpacks and headed for the nearest tube stop.

"Are you ladies coming with us? We're going to the police station to file a report," the Vegas grandma called out to them.

"No, we're looking for a cyber café," Megan said.

"Oh good idea! A letter-writing campaign! Are you alerting the media?"

"Not exactly. But we wish you the best of luck!"

"Yes, have a safe trip home!" Megan added as they headed down the street.

"You think anyone will believe them?" Julianna asked.

"I don't know. I'm so tired, and I can't think about it anymore."

Setting aside their sleuthing for the moment and using their guidebooks, they located a cyber café near their hotel, figured out how to buy the time they needed to access their email accounts, and sat down. Several coffees and forty-five minutes later, they were both caught up with friends and family and ready for the comforts of their hotel.

"I feel guilty lying to them," Megan said.

"You know they'd become completely unhinged," Julianna said, pushing out of the café door and heading to the corner. "If we're not going to report this to the authorities, then we can't report it at all, you know?"

"Agreed. But let's watch the news and the local papers and see if any of the other passengers gets the story out."

"Good idea."

They headed toward the hotel, too tired to keep up

with the pace of the other walkers.

"We must look wonderful," Megan said.

"Oh yeah, I think we're scaring children," Julianna laughed. Neither had been able to brush their hair. Julianna's, which was long and straight, was hanging in limp, slightly greasy knots. Megan's, much shorter, was matted to the back of her head, the tufts spiking out randomly. Neither would be making an appearance in a fashion magazine anytime soon. Julianna had pulled a jacket out of her pack to cover her blood-soaked t-shirt, but scarlet splatters still marked her jeans and sneakers, adding to their overall startling look.

They reached the hotel and walked in, trudging across the fancy lobby and causing more than a few eyebrows to rise.

"May I help you?" asked the clerk, probably afraid they were about to hold up the place.

"We're guests here. Room 562," Megan said, a little testy, as she produced a key for proof.

"Oh, Room 562? I think you have a message." The clerk reached for an envelope on the rear counter. "You're Julianna Wright?"

"That's me," Julianna replied, excited enough to wake up a little. She took the envelope and rewarded the clerk with a big smile. Staring at the unfamiliar handwriting, she followed Megan to the elevator.

They arrived at their room in silence, Julianna clutching the envelope tightly, her eyes riveted to the masculine script. *Could that be Nat's writing?* she wondered, unwilling to break the spell by opening it quite yet.

Megan tossed her backpack down. "Dibs on the bathroom," she said, heading for it.

Julianna removed her backpack, too. Then she sat

down on her bed, slowly opened the envelope with one finger and drew out the slip of paper inside. Hotel stationery, she noted idly, closing her eyes for a moment and inhaling deeply before letting the air out slowly. Finally, she opened her eyes again and began to read—

Jersey,

I'm so sorry I had to disappear and leave you there. You know I can't explain. But we're not done talking. Please don't be mad.

Love,

N.

She smiled at that. *Love?* There was that word again. Did he really mean it? How *could* he? They barely knew each other. Still, he'd somehow already worked his way into her heart. But how deep were those feelings? And how could the two of them build anything together if he just disappeared whenever he wanted, with little or no explanation?

Then something else occurred to her: *How did he find out where Megan and I were staying in the first place?*

She sighed. All of it was probably just part of his job and his life. Would she ever grow accustomed to the constant intrigue and worry?

She glanced down at the note again, realizing there was a line at the very end she hadn't read.

PS—Your bliss theory's a load of crap.

The doubts and questions were still there, but she couldn't stop her answering smile.

Chapter 13

A Face in the Crowd

THE ROOM WAS DARK when Julianna finally awoke.

At first there was confusion, like always. Then it became replaced with memories.

The hotel.

She was back safe in the hotel. And Nat…he seemed to think he loved her.

Mmm.

She stretched happily, turning to see if her sister was still asleep.

"Meg?" she whispered.

"Yeah, I'm here," Megan said with a yawn. "We just slept the whole day away. We're never going to get rid of our jet lag now."

"I know. And now our plans are totally ruined. We were supposed to go to the British Museum. And have tea. And see a play. That was our itinerary today."

"Well, we've got to go do *something*," Meg said. "Or we're going to be the only London tourists in history who didn't make it to a single landmark."

"At least we've saved a lot of money," Julianna said. "Okay, let's get up. Maybe we can find some dinner and walk around a little."

The thought of a hot shower sounded heavenly as she padded toward the bathroom. How was it possible to be having such a failure of a vacation and still feel so happy?

After they both showered, dressed, and dried their hair, they grabbed their jackets and packs and headed for the door. It was already past seven, and they were starving.

They reached the street and arbitrarily chose a direction, taking in the sights, sounds, and smells of the beautiful city. The trademark red, double-decker buses crowded the busy streets, along with the black taxicabs. They walked to the nearest bus stop, then chose the first one that would take them to Piccadilly Circus, a more populated area filled with restaurants.

"What do you think?" Julianna asked, spotting a pub. "Wanna just give that one a try?"

"What? You mean you didn't research this in the guidebook?" Megan teased. "I'm shocked."

"I got a little distracted. But tomorrow we can pick up where we left off."

They jumped from the bus as soon as it stopped, and the pub they'd spotted turned out to be filled with riotous laughter. Televisions were hung around the circular wooden bar at the center of the room. A crowd of young men in colorfully striped shirts were engrossed in a soccer game—*it's football here,* Julianna reminded herself. Their team must have scored, because the men erupted in shouts of back-slapping happiness.

"Look, Jules, authentic football fans," Megan commented just under the din. "Mark that off our must-see list."

"Fans. Check," Julianna said as she surveyed the rest of the room in mild confusion. Were they supposed to just claim one of the dark, wooden booths along the perimeter, or was someone supposed to seat them?

Finally, a harried-looking woman took pity on them and indicated a booth by the front window, which provided a great view of the busy sidewalk. They smiled gratefully and headed for their seats, picking up two rather sticky menus and anxiously scanning them.

"Hmm, what sounds good, do you think?" Megan asked.

"I don't know about you, but I'm too tired to make such a difficult decision."

"Isn't it some sort of law that you have to order fish and chips your first time in an English pub?"

"Oh, right. Good point." Julianna laid the menu back down with a laugh. "What a relief."

After they placed their orders, Julianna whipped out her guidebook. "Let's see what we're doing tomorrow," she said, also pulling out the itinerary.

"Aren't we going shopping in Notting Hill?"

"Yep, in the afternoon. But first we're going to the Tower of London, which is clear across town. Why did we plan it that way?"

"I don't know. So we'd have an excuse to stop for a nap in the hotel?"

"Oh yeah, okay. That works for me. Let's see...."

Julianna flipped back to the index to find the right page number, then thumbed through the book until she found the information about the tower. "Wow, did you know the first stone for the tower was laid in 1078?"

"Prepping for *Jeopardy*?"

"Just trying to get into this vacation. Okay, it says here they give guided tours everyday starting at nine."

"I think we can get moving that early," Megan replied, taking a sip of her soda and making a face. "Why are all the drinks here warm? Are we guarding the ice recipe too closely?"

"Nat!" Julianna said a little too loudly, ignoring her sister's comment as she gazed excitedly at the crowd of people walking past them outside.

"Huh?" Megan asked.

"I just saw him, I'm sure of it!" she said jumping up from their table. "I'll be back!"

She rounded the corner by the front, slowing just long enough to avoid knocking over a startled waitress before she slammed her hands into the heavy, wooden door and knocked it roughly open. Then she burst onto the sidewalk and started her pursuit, dodging the bystanders as much as she could while trying to pick out the blue Yankees cap that had caught her eye.

She kept up this frantic pace for a couple blocks, glad the lights seemed to be timed in her favor. She couldn't believe the sea of people she was working her way through—where was everyone headed at this time of the evening? And she still hadn't caught sight of him again. *How could he have disappeared so quickly?*

Eventually she had to slow down, the stitch in her side finally forcing her to stop and catch her breath. As she stood panting on the sidewalk, she turned in a slow circle, trying to catch a glimpse of him. Frustrated with his disappearing act and mad at herself for getting emotional and teary for what seemed like the millionth time in only two days, she turned back toward the pub in defeat.

"Jerk," she muttered, not certain if that was aimed at Nat or herself. She angrily wiped away a tear with one hand, then caught a reflection in a storefront window that made her spin around rapidly. There, directly across the street with his back to her, stood a tall man in jeans and a long-sleeved blue sweatshirt. He also had a blue baseball cap on his head.

"Nat!" she called, racing into the street. A taxi driver skidded to a halt in front of her. She forgot the traffic pattern was just opposite of what she was used to—the cab had approached her from the right, and she hadn't even bothered looking in that direction.

"I'm sorry," she called to him, slowing her pace to watch for other cars. *Me getting mowed down in traffic is just what this trip needs to make it complete*, she thought.

After navigating the remainder of the busy street and irate drivers, she ran up to Nat, who still had his back to her as he looked in a Boots Pharmacy store window. *What's the fascination?* she thought with mild irritation. Those stores were practically on every block in London.

"Nat!" she said, putting her hand on his arm. "Where have you been?"

Startled out of his reverie, he turned around.

"Do I know you?" asked the man, a complete stranger, in the distinct local accent.

"Oh, I'm so sorry!" she said to the man who, she now saw, had vividly blond hair. "I thought you were someone else. My apologies...."

She turned back in the direction of the pub without waiting for a response. She couldn't help it; this was all too much. The embarrassment of almost getting run over in order to accost a stranger, the intense disappointment of not finding Nat, her lack of food and sleep, and of course the hostage situation...and now tears were flowing freely down her face, too.

Chapter 14

Questions and Tears

DEVASTATED, she made her way back to the pub, careful to cross the street at the light this time.

She walked back inside and slid into the booth, thoroughly embarrassed.

Megan looked up from her plate and considered her sister's teary face. "The good news is the cod is delicious," she said.

That made Julianna laugh. She pulled a tissue out of her backpack and wiped her eyes, struggling to regain control of her emotions.

"What's the bad news?" Megan asked softly. "You didn't find him, or you *did* find him, and he's a jerk?"

"No, I found the guy I saw. It just wasn't Nat. He didn't even look anything like him. I'm such an idiot."

"Why? Because you went running after a guy? Or maybe because you're maybe falling in love for the first time and don't know what to do about it? Or is it because your food's cold?"

"Yes. All of the above, I guess," Julianna said, settling her napkin in her lap and picking up her fork, determined to pull herself together.

"Aahh. So you *are* falling in love with him?" Megan asked.

"What, now you're giving me trick questions?" Julianna was a little annoyed at herself for showing her feelings for Nat. Perhaps she should just take out a full-page ad in the *London Times* and be done with it.

"I'm happy for you, you jerk," Megan said, smiling into her older sister's red, puffy eyes.

"Yeah, this is terrific. I maybe fall in love for the first time, only to have the guy ditch me in the middle of a hostage situation. Makes me want to write a sonnet." Julianna idly pushed the pieces of increasingly cold fish around her plate with her fork. "And here's what really makes me mad: I went on this vacation to take charge of my life, right?"

"And to accrue frequent flier miles?"

"That too. But mostly I was marking a whole new part of my life and a whole new me: A Julianna who no longer merely lives her life through everyone else. And now here I am, a few days into the trip, completely destroyed by some guy. I'm letting Nat—well, okay, and some terrorists—totally wreck this trip and get me all upset. So much for the new Julianna." Her voice cracked at the end.

Megan looked up, and Julianna could feel tears forming in her eyes again.

Megan put her fork down and leaned back in her chair. "That is such a load of crap," she said, folding her arms and staring.

"What?" Julianna asked. "What's a load of crap? The fact that I'm getting jerked around by Super Spy?"

"No. Your little theory that you've let other people run your life is. *That's* the load of crap."

"No it's not!" Julianna said, feeling increasingly angry now. "All I do is go to work and make guest appearances in everyone else's life. I depend on you and Mom and Dad and my girlfriends for everything, including emotional support, love, and entertainment. What do I ever do alone and for myself? The most independent thing I ever did was move out of the house and find an apartment. And we even did *that* together!"

"Are you done feeling sorry for yourself?" Megan asked. "Because that's not the way I see it at all. You have lived—and continue to live—your life precisely the way *you want to.* You were never ready to look for all the other stuff people want—love, marriage, children, homeownership, and whatever else we're talking about here. If you're ready for it all now, I think that's terrific; I really do. But just give yourself a little bit of a break and admit that, until now, you've been pretty darn happy."

"What about the bridesmaid blur? Do you know how much money and time I've wasted on silk shantung and matching fake pearl accessories? How exactly was I taking charge of my life when I didn't stop saying yes to that whole scene around weddings three and four?"

"Oh, give me a break! You were just being you—a really, incredibly generous and loving friend. If you had all three hundred of them to do over again, you wouldn't change a thing!"

"No. You're wrong. I would have picked out a different strapless bra for wedding seven," Julianna said with a smirk, breaking the tension that was building between them. "That thing really dug into my side."

"Okay, aside from that horrendous screwup, admit you've been having fun," Megan said, clearly not ready to let the topic drop.

"Meg, all it's done is make me not want to get married."

"Why?!"

"Because so many of those weddings have led first to miserable marriages and then to the inevitable divorces. It doesn't matter how much money the bride and groom spent on the wedding, how many tiers the cake had, or how perfect the weather was. It's all a joke." Then Julianna added, "Not to mention a crapshoot."

"That's really what's bothering you, isn't it? You want some sort of guarantee that a big poofy wedding will automatically equal a long, happy marriage like Mom and Dad's. Am I right?"

"Well, it sounds dumb when you put it like that," Julianna said in a teasing tone, still trying to lighten the mood.

"It *is* dumb, Jules. Your friends have made some mistakes. How? Why? Because they took chances, and they just lived their lives? So you're going to shut yourself off from commitment and children and happiness because you're afraid to make the same mistakes?"

Tears started to fall down Julianna's face again. "I'm sorry," she said, digging for another tissue. "I don't know why I'm such a crybaby suddenly."

"Is it because I hit on the truth, and you're avoiding admitting it? Listen, you don't have to tell me if I'm right, because I know I am. That's because *I know you*, Jules. And you might find this shocking since I just bullied you into tears, but I love you, too. I just want you to be happy. So quit pretending you're not in charge of your life. And if you're really falling for Nat, then don't you dare let him get away."

"I'd have to find him before I could prevent him from leaving again," Julianna said with a laugh at the wickedly expectant face Megan was making. "Okay, yes. You're right. You're right about Nat anyway. I *do* want to find a way to make it work with him."

"Then my work here is done," Megan replied, smiling for the first time since the conversation turned so serious. She leaned back toward the table and grabbed her fork again. "Just think about the other things I said too, okay?"

"Yes, I promise. Now quit being such a pit bull."

"Fine," Megan agreed. "But you know I can't stand it when something doesn't make sense."

"Yeah, yeah," Julianna muttered, pulling her money out of her bag. Megan was right about one thing for sure—nothing in her life had made sense since she met Nat.

Now she was afraid if she didn't see him again, nothing ever would.

Chapter 15

Rethinking

JULIANNA WAS RELIEVED that Megan seemed lost in her own thoughts as they walked back to their hotel. She was tired of thinking and talking and analyzing and, especially, crying. Their short time in London had been an emotional roller coaster so far, and she was ready to get off the ride.

They trudged wearily across the lobby for the second time that day. The bus trip seemed like a lifetime ago, she mused. At least they didn't look like refugees upon their return this time.

As they passed by the front desk, she couldn't stop herself from asking whether there were any messages for her. She managed a quick *Thanks anyway* when the bubbly woman working behind the desk said no.

As disappointment flooded through her, Julianna gave herself a mental kick. *What's wrong with me, anyway?* Even *she* was getting annoyed with her moping. No wonder Megan had ripped into her. After all, Nat's note had said they weren't done talking, which meant he wanted to see her again, too. He probably meant after they got back to the United States. In fact, he probably thought they flew home right after the whole hostage fiasco. Maybe *he* had even gone home since the situation had wrapped up so neatly.

That last thought didn't do a thing to cheer her up as she sullenly followed Megan into the room. Still silent, the pair went through the motions of calling it a day even though they'd only been awake a few short hours.

"Good night," Megan said as she climbed into her bed.

"Yeah, good night," Julianna said. "Oh, and Meg?"

"Yes?"

"Thank you," she said. "For everything."

"Any time," Megan said with a smile before rolling over to face the opposite wall.

*   *   *

Julianna yawned and lay back on her pillow, thinking over everything Megan had said at the pub. *Maybe I really am being an idiot about the whole marriage and wedding thing.* What, really, did her girlfriends' choices have to do with her anyway? Had her hatred of marriage just been a pink-taffeta cover she'd neatly draped over her fears? Was she lying to herself or trying to simplify a more complex issue?

Another thought crossed her mind, making her cringe as it popped its way through her tangle of worries—

Maybe all along what I've really been terrified of is not finding someone to love—or someone who could love me. Could the bridesmaid excuse have been a subconscious way of masking that fear? She could feel her face flush with embarrassment. If that last idea was true, then she was the least self-aware person ever born. All it had taken was one day with Nat and his sappy ideas about love and marriage, and suddenly the prospect of having those things in her life was tantalizing?

Megan's right, I am an idiot.

No—it would take more than that to completely rewrite her every idea about love and marriage. Ideas that took thirty years to form shouldn't be tossed aside after a few kisses with a stranger who claimed to work for the CIA—and one deep talk with a too-smart little sister.

Julianna rolled over to get more comfortable and a little more serious about getting some decent sleep.

I should focus on seeing Nat for the second time before I worry about whether I'm going to marry him, she thought ruefully, finally forcing the topic to drop from her thoughts.

For that night, anyway.

Chapter 16

Attempting to Relax and Forget

"NOPE, NOTHING. Not one word," Megan said, setting down the copy of the *London Times* she'd been reading.

"Yeah, nothing about it in *The Guardian*, *The Observer*, or *The Independent*, either," Julianna replied, setting them all on the table. "I guess we were right that someone really didn't want this story to get out."

"I've been thinking about that, and I wonder if maybe we we're *over*thinking it. The CIA probably just doesn't want anyone to know it's got agents in town. And they probably just didn't want to scare anyone needlessly, either."

"Yeah, you could be right, I guess."

Julianna dove into her breakfast. Since she'd spent more time at the pub the night before crying than eating, she was ravenous, so she had ordered a big traditional English breakfast: fried eggs, bacon, sausage, beans, and toast.

They got out their maps and planned their route to the Tower of London, which was across town in the financial district and next to the famous Tower Bridge. Then they finished eating, paid their bill, and headed for the nearest tube stop.

As they made their way across town, Julianna couldn't help searching for Nat's gorgeous face. *Will I ever be able to get him off my mind?* she asked herself, then was instantly depressed by the question. She had been determined not to let anything ruin her trip. Yet now, barely a few days into it, she was already distracted and sulky. *He said we'd talk again,* she reminded herself. He also had said he'd look her up when he got home. So, in the meantime, she decided she needed to pull herself together, attempt to enjoy her vacation, and *relax.*

The mental pep talk was surprisingly effective. By the time they emerged from the Tube and got in line for tickets, she was back in a happy, positive frame of mind and ready to be a tourist again.

The Tower of London was actually a group of buildings, including a huge castle, a chapel, and some actual towers, surrounded by green grass and daffodils where a moat had once encircled the famous prison and royal palace. The beauty of the site couldn't help but continue to brighten Julianna's mood even further. The tour was conducted by a relentlessly cheerful "Beefeater"—a retired member of the royal guard. He led the large group from building to building, happily recalling for the crowd the countless deaths and imprisonments that had made the tower so famous.

"Maybe this doom and gloom wasn't the best idea today," Megan whispered.

"There's a pretty bloody history here," Julianna replied. "But at least it's taking my mind off you know who."

"Well, gee, I'm sure that'd make all the beheaded prisoners feel better, knowing they'd at least get to distract you one day."

"Very funny," Julianna said. "You know what I mean. Despite everything that's happened, this trip is just what I needed."

"Well, that's good," Megan told her.

They finished the guided tour, then followed the

group into one of the buildings to view the crown jewels—a large collection of royal crowns and scepters—then ended with a walk through the White Tower; a castle built when William the Conqueror was the ruler of England. It was filled with displays of ancient arms and armor. Finally, they crossed the pedestrian bridge over the former moat and headed to the gift shop.

Julianna sighed happily and thought, *Yeah, it's possible.* She really could do it—she could actually put Nat out of her mind and enjoy herself.

For the first time since the gunmen overtook their bus en route to their stop in Bath, this trip finally felt like it was going to be okay.

Chapter 17

Another Incident

LEAVING MEGAN to finish rooting through the gift shop, Julianna walked outside and took a deep breath. She was still pleased with herself for getting away from the black cloud she'd been stuck under since Nat had entered her life—and then disappeared from it. Now she was once more determined to really enjoy this vacation for exactly what it was: a chance to see a new part of the world, relax, and have fun.

She wandered farther away from the gift shop and through an iron gate, taking in the sights all around her and pulling out her umbrella when she noticed a few drops of rain on the sleeves of her jacket.

The Tower was located in the financial heart of London. Hundreds of well-dressed professionals milling around during their lunch hour blended with the tourists still lining up for the tour.

She glanced back toward the gift shop, but there was still no sign of Megan. So she continued walking along the sidewalk toward the busy crowds. As she went, the sound of raised voices shook her out of her reverie. She went in that direction out of sheer curiosity, although she was mostly still caught up in her own thoughts.

The scene that awaited her snapped her mind back into full focus. A man with a large, bulky backpack was running down the street. People were yelling and horns were sounding as he weaved in and out of the cars, then jumped up on the sidewalk, barreling into a crowd of tourists.

What's he running from? Julianna wondered as he continued knocking people aside to make his way up the sidewalk—and right into her path. She jumped back with a gasp before he could reach her, flattening herself against the stone wall she was walking along. He raced past and directly toward the gift shop. She could see the sweat on his face and hear his panting breaths.

Before he reached the gate to the shop, Julianna finally realized what he was running from. Two black, unmarked cars flew down the street, brakes squealing as they drove toward him. Then eight men jumped out and grabbed for their weapons.

More guns, Julianna realized, and was suddenly sorry she'd wandered so far from her sister. Where *was* she, anyway? She hoped Megan would stay safely inside the gift shop until whatever was currently happening was over.

When the running man reached the gates, Julianna guessed he'd quickly disappear from sight with the lead he had, but her mouth fell open in shock as he stopped and turned back around, a gun she hadn't noticed originally now evident in his hands.

I could get shot, she realized, her confusion melting away with this suddenly clear realization. In not retreating immediately, Julianna had put herself directly in the path of danger.

Even as fear struck her in that moment of clarity, she could hear the men from the car shout a warning. When the man with the gun didn't drop his weapon, one of the men by the cars pulled up a gun of his own, steadied his aim, and—after one more shouted warning—pulled the trigger.

Onlookers screamed as the man with the backpack fell, shot once.

Julianna gasped, covering her mouth with her hand to smother the scream that was building in her chest and throat. What was going on? Was he hit in the chest, arm, or head? It had happened too fast for Julianna to know for certain. And was the man dead or just wounded? She couldn't tell.

The men from the cars swarmed around him, along with policemen who had suddenly appeared and were quickly erecting a barricade, all of which blocked the fallen man from her view. In disbelief, Julianna turned her attention back to the shooter. As that man calmly put his gun back in his holster and then turned to say something to one of his colleagues, Julianna gasped.

Nat....

It was him. He had shot the man with the backpack.

*   *   *

Her thoughts were a complete jumble. Horror at what she just witnessed blurred together with her relief at seeing Nat again. He was safe and healthy. He was still in London and apparently still chasing terrorists.

She tried to return her focus to the scene. *If the CIA is involved, then that man is probably a terrorist.* What was he going to do? Shoot tourists? Blow up the Tower? Or maybe the famous Tower Bridge that crossed the Thames River on the opposite side of the Tower from where she was standing. That would certainly get people's attention.

She was now completely frantic about where Megan was. How did they keep getting into these situations? And, as a nurse, shouldn't she go offer whatever help she could give to the man who'd been shot?

An ambulance pulled up just then, ending at least that part of the dilemma for her. She wasn't sure how she would have felt about tending a wound she had just seen Nat inflict anyway, and instead she allowed herself to be a silent bystander. Policemen finished setting up the barricade around the scene, which now stood between Julianna and the gift shop where she hoped her sister was still located. Meanwhile, she stood rooted to the spot, her eyes locked on Nat. Despite everything that had just happened—or maybe despite everything that had *almost* happened—she still couldn't help being swept up in the emotions of seeing him.

He was wearing jeans just like the first time she had seen him, but the baseball cap was gone and so was the t-shirt. A white, long-sleeved shirt was in its place, the top few buttons undone to show a hint of his chest. *Mmm....* She dreamily remembered how wonderful it felt to lean against that chest and be held by those strong arms.

Then she realized with a start how inappropriate her train of thought truly was right now.

"What's wrong with me?" she whispered to herself in horror. Nat had just shot a man—maybe even killed him, in fact—and all she could do was drool over his chest.

She didn't know if she should be horror-stricken by his actions or maybe even be afraid of him. *Yeah, that's what I need—more to be confused about*, she thought.

The rain started to fall harder as the ambulance carrying the wounded man pulled away. Police dogs were sniffing the backpack, and more cars were coming to the scene.

Bomb squad? she mused, although the terrifying possibilities of just what that backpack contained still hadn't made her move or shift her gaze away from Nat.

The CIA team started returning to their cars.

No! she thought wildly. *You can't leave yet!*

As though he sensed her presence—or maybe just her panic—Nat stopped talking to the others and slowly turned toward her, his eyes finally meeting hers. Despite the distance between them, Julianna could see the shock on his face. He didn't move, either. And he looked as mesmerized as she felt.

They stood that way, lost in each other's eyes, for what felt like hours. In reality, it was probably only a few short seconds. The rain continued to fall, soaking Nat's white shirt and outlining the contours of his muscles, Julianna couldn't help noticing.

Finally, Nat broke the impasse between them by slowly raising his right hand, his fingers forming the familiar sign.

I love you.

He held it for a moment, then lowered his arm again, still staring. Without breaking her gaze, she smiled broadly at him.

Go team, she signed in response.

He just shook his head and smiled.

I should tell him, she decided. Despite her fears and hang-ups, and the impossibly confusing set of circumstances they were caught up in, she owed him the truth: She was falling for him too. Nat deserved as much honesty and candor *from* her as he was willingly giving *to* her.

As she started to raise her hand again, her fingers about to sign a more honest reply, one of the men said something to Nat, breaking his concentration as well as their gaze. The spell that had woven itself between them melted away.

Julianna regretfully dropped her hand as Nat said something in response to the man. Then he looked back at her, his own regret evident on his face.

"No!" Julianna yelled, running toward the barricade as Nat ducked his head down and climbed into the backseat of the black car. "Don't go!"

The door slammed shut, and the car sped away.

*   *   *

Her panic was quickly replaced by frustration and regret. She silently watched the car drive down the street and away from the scene.

And away from me.

The black windows in the car blocked her view, so she didn't know if Nat was still watching her. Were they ever going to be able to do something as normal as talk on the phone or go on a date? She seriously doubted it.

Sighing and trying to shake off her melancholy, she turned around and headed back toward the barricade, which was still blocking the visitors trying to exit the gift shop. She'd have to wait, which would give her an opportunity to try to force herself to forget what had just happened, something she was determined to do. She had a sister to find and a vacation to enjoy—even if it killed her.

Chapter 18

Notting Hill

THE MORNING and most of the afternoon were gone by the time they were allowed past the police barricade, forced to wait for the authorities to untangle the messy scene from which Nat had so quickly vanished. *Had it only been a few short hours ago?* she thought.

"What in the world is going on?" Megan asked, the frustration abundantly evident on her face. "Why can't we tour just one site without it becoming a national crisis?"

"Yeah, well, it's a personal crisis, too," Julianna said. "Did you see who shot that man?"

"No, I didn't see anything, although I heard someone had been shot. I've been trapped in a room filled with postcards of the Queen, Beefeater key chains, and lavender-scented bath products. What happened?"

"I'll tell you as we walk. I'm starving again. Come on...."

She recounted the morning's mysterious events, although she edited out the part about Nat telling her he loved her while she stood there staring like a deer in the headlights and totally missing her chance to tell him she might just love him, too. Julianna just couldn't bring herself to discuss it yet—the overwhelming feeling of seeing him again, only to have him disappear once more. It was still too raw.

"Wow, Jules, I'm sorry," Megan said. They were back on the Tube now, heading in the direction of their hotel. They planned to walk around the Notting Hill section of the city, looking for a late lunch and some good shopping.

Julianna shrugged, trying to act indifferent. "He was just doing his job," she said.

"Yeah, okay. And he might have actually taken a life in the course of that job. And then, by the way, he just vanished again without saying a word to you. Yeah, you're right, that's no big deal at all."

"Back off, Meg, please," Julianna said, fighting to maintain her calm. "It sucks, okay? You're right. There, I've said it. This whole thing absolutely sucks. But there's not a single thing I can do about it, so I'm choosing to focus on the fact that at least I know he's okay. I may not know where he is, and I may have witnessed something pretty horrible, but at least I know he's *okay*. And I know this sounds crazy, but that's enough for right now. It really is."

Doubt was clear on Megan's face, although she tried to mask it for Julianna's sake. "Yeah, Jules, you're right. That *is* a good thing. I'm glad Nat's okay, and I'm glad you got to see him again."

"Thanks," Julianna said softly, smiling at last.

*　　*　　*

They got to Notting Hill around three, had a quick lunch of sandwiches and tea at a café, then discussed where to shop. Megan was dying to hit the bookstores, but Julianna wanted to hunt for antiques. So they decided to split up, planning to meet back at the Travel Bookstore in two hours.

Julianna wandered down Portobello Road, window-shopping until she found a store that caught her attention. She opened the door, smiling at the quaint sound of the little bell as she entered. She walked through the displays of old furniture, costume jewelry, and dusty clothing, glad for the chance to exercise a little retail therapy. *Shopping always helps*, she thought.

The bell sounded again as another customer walked in. With her back to the door, Julianna felt, rather than heard, the person approach her.

And then a familiar voice said softly, "Hey Jersey."

Chapter 19

The Bracelet

JULIANNA JUMPED, startled enough to drop the silver bracelet she'd been admiring.

"Let me," Nat said, leaning over to pick it up.

She watched him out of the corner of her eye, afraid of how intense her emotions were. Could she even survive looking into those beautiful blue eyes again?

He stood back up and offered the bracelet to her, his arm extended in an invitation.

Julianna turned around but kept her eyes down, focusing on the bracelet and unable to say anything to him or even meet his gaze. *Why is this so awkward?* she thought, as she finally reached out.

The moment her fingers wrapped around the bracelet, Nat quickly used his other hand to capture hers. The warmth of his body surged through her, along with the now-familiar electricity that she had felt each time they'd touched.

She couldn't avoid it any longer. Slowly she ran her gaze up his body—he'd changed into a different shirt, this one a light yellow, and he'd dried off, too—and he looked as sexy as ever. Finally, her eyes finished their journey past his chiseled chin and full lips and locked with his own.

"Yellow's a great color on you," she said, wondering in passing if there were any contests she could enter for bad opening lines.

"Are you okay?" he asked, concern marking his features. He dropped his right hand from its hold on the bracelet, slowly lifting his fingers to touch her cheek with a feathery, delicate caress. He brushed back a strand of her hair, tucking it behind her ear. His other hand still encircled hers.

She felt as though she couldn't breathe in that moment. *The electricity surging through my body could run a factory for a week*, she thought.

"Yes, I'm okay," she whispered. "Are you?"

"I'm great now," Nat said. "I shouldn't have come, but I just couldn't wait to see you again. Not after what happened before."

"After what *keeps* happening, you mean?" she asked, pleased that her skills of speech and cognition had suddenly checked back in. "Seems like someone gets shot every time we're together."

"I'm so sorry you had to see that," Nat said. "But you know he would have killed us all if given the chance, right?"

"I don't know anything anymore," Julianna confessed. "I've never been so confused, so miserable, and at the same time so wildly happy in my life. Does that make any sense?"

"Yes," Nat said, nodding. "Yes, it does."

He knows precisely what I mean, she realized. He was looking at her so seriously and so intently. You'd think he was apologizing for shooting *her*.

"Let's get out of here before the shopkeeper starts to wonder just what we're doing with that bracelet," Nat suggested. "Do you want it?"

"Yes," she said, knowing she could never part with it now. Reluctantly, she pulled her hand from his, then reached for her money.

"Please, let me. It's the least I can do after everything I've put you through," Nat said, taking out his wallet.

"That's not necessary," she said, abandoning the argument after catching the wounded look on his face. "Well, okay...then thank you. Now I'll always think of you when I wear it."

"That's the idea," Nat told her, walking over to the counter.

She watched him make the transaction, amazed again at how insanely happy she felt when she was with him. The confusion and tears of the last few days were nothing more than a hazy bad memory. Her every thought and feeling were now in sharp focus, and nothing except this beautiful, wonderful man seemed important at all.

He turned around and headed back to her side. She smiled and sighed with contentment.

He took her hand, gently hooking the bracelet, with its tiny purple beads and silver links, onto her wrist. The action, which she'd performed herself a million times on her own, felt heart-stoppingly sensual when *he* did it.

"It's beautiful, just like you, Jersey," he said, taking her hand once more and lacing their fingers together.

"Are you trying to sweet-talk me, Super Spy?"

"Yes," he replied. "Why? Is it working?"

"I'll let you know," she said with a smile as they walked out of the shop together and onto the crowded sidewalk.

Chapter 20

Making His Feelings Clear

"WHERE'S MEGAN?" Nat asked as they started walking.

"We split up for the time being. She's busy rooting through bookstores, and I wanted to check out the antiques."

"How long before you're supposed to meet up with her?"

"Another hour or so, why?"

"Let's go find someplace where we can talk, okay?"

"Sure. Lead the way...."

They walked hand-in-hand for several blocks, admiring the little shops that lined the streets. The crooked, tightly packed buildings seemed to be desperately hanging onto each other for support. They could quite easily find a future modeling for the dictionary definition of *quaint*. Much of the area's commerce seemed to be happening on tables set up on the sidewalk, giving a street-fair feeling to the area.

Eventually they found a little corner café, where they ordered tea—"It's a law," Nat informed her—then they picked out a little table in the back.

Nat pulled the chair out for her, which was almost Julianna's undoing.

"And manners too, huh?" she asked, sliding her backpack off and settling it at her feet as she sat.

"I'm not always a total jerk, you know," he replied, taking the seat across from her.

Julianna smiled and picked up her white teacup. She tried to take a sip, but the hot liquid burned her lips and mouth, so much so that she set the cup back down with a clatter.

"You okay?" he asked.

"Mmm, sorry. I think they heat the tea here in an atom splitter. What was the flavor, isotope?"

"Well, at least you haven't lost your sense of humor," Nat observed, heeding her warning and setting down his own cup.

She couldn't take it anymore. She had to cut through the politeness and find out if what he was feeling—what he was *telling* her he was feeling, anyway—was real. And she needed to know right away, afraid if she didn't find out, he'd vanish again.

"Did you mean what you said?" she blurted out before truly considering what she was going to say.

Nat seemed completely unfazed by her outburst. *Does anything surprise him—ever?* she wondered.

"Depends. What did I say?"

"That you, well, you know, that you..." her voice trailed off as her nerve faltered. "Never mind. I'm an idiot."

"That I love you?" he asked gently, smiling as she nodded awkwardly in reply. "Yes, with my whole heart."

"How is that possible? How is any of this possible? We just met each other, and here you are, completely turning my life inside out."

"I don't know how or why it's true. It just is."

"Does this happen a lot?"

"Do you mean do I make it a habit of saying *I love you* to all the beautiful women I pick up while on duty? No, no I don't. In fact, this is a complete first."

"The first time you've met someone you're interested in while on duty, you mean?"

"Well, yes. But I meant it's the first time I've been in love. Really, truly, knock-me-on-the-ground, knew-it-right-away, wouldn't-dare-dream-of-being-without-you-another-minute love."

"Um...okay. Wow."

When she gazed in his eyes, she saw nothing but honesty there. Once again, he was giving her everything straight from his heart, and she was giving him nothing in return.

She looked down, pretending to have a fascination with the lava in her teacup while she collected her thoughts. She really had to tell him that he wasn't the only one who felt this way. In fact, he'd pretty much summed up precisely how *she* was feeling. They were definitely in this together, and he deserved to know.

She took a deep breath and looked up, finally prepared to lay her cards on the table, too.

"And that's why," Nat cut in, halting her confession, "I really have to insist that you go home."

Chapter 21

Getting the Last Word

TAKEN OFF GUARD, Julianna could only stare at him in shock.

"It's just too dangerous here," he continued. "I told you we had information that terrorists were targeting tourists, and I think you can attest firsthand that our information was pretty solid."

"Yes, but...."

He put a hand up. "You're going to say that the United States is every bit as dangerous right now. Right?"

"Well, yes. You live in New York. You saw what happened there on 9/11 just like I did. Who's to say it can't happen again?" She was starting to get upset now, in part because of this radical change in topic, but also because she didn't need him telling her how to live her life, his love notwithstanding.

"Our intelligence says something different at the moment," Nat said. He reached across the table and captured her hand in his, squeezing it as he continued. "And I can't do my job if I'm worried day and night about you and where you are."

"You always seem to know right where I am," she snapped, a scowl on her face. "So just avoid me."

"The only reason I was able to find you today is because I remembered the itinerary. Shopping in Notting Hill was on the same day as the Tower of London. I teased you about the itinerary, remember?

Thursday is your scheduled free time?"

"Yes," she said, still frowning. "You have a frighteningly accurate memory."

"And if I know you're here," he continued as if she hadn't spoken, "then I don't think I *can* avoid you. And I know I can't stop thinking about you."

"I can't stop thinking about you, either. But I don't want to leave you here. And before you protest, I already know what you're going to say. It's too dangerous. And you're working, so we really can't spend any time together anyhow. Fine."

"Is that, *Fine, I'll go home where I can be safe*, or *Fine, I'm too stubborn to know when something's for my own good?*" Nat asked.

"No, neither of those. It's more like, *Fine, say whatever you want, but I'm a big girl, and I've successfully lived thirty years without your tutelage, so I think I can make it another week.*"

"Did you just use the word *tutelage* in a sentence?" Nat asked, clearly trying to lighten the mood.

"Yes, shall I wow you with more of my verbal prowess? Oh, that's right!" she smacked her forehead to increase the sarcasm. "We can't see each other or talk or exchange phone numbers or be in any other way a normal couple. No, we just make out, issue commands, count the bodies, and disappear on each other!"

"So, are you actually refusing to go?" Nat said, his voice echoing the same anger she felt. He stopped talking and took in a deep breath, running his fingers through his curls before he exhaled slowly. "Jersey, I'm not commanding you here. I know I don't have that right. But please, *please* think about it."

"And I'm not trying to be a pain. But I paid for this vacation out of my own hard-earned money, and so far it's been a complete bust. I just want to see a few historical landmarks before I go home!" Other patrons were starting to stare at them, so she lowered her voice to a whispered hiss. "Nat, think about it. There are probably two million other tourists in London as we speak, give or take a million. What *really* are the odds that *I'll* be the one who gets hurt?"

"Whatever the odds are, they're too high," he replied firmly, releasing her hand and leaning back in his chair.

"So now you're mad at me?"

"Yes, I think you're being stubborn and unreasonable and foolish and...."

"All right, I get it! But I'm not leaving, and I can't believe how stubborn *you're* being about this! If you have specific information about a certain spot I should avoid, then just tell me," she challenged.

"You know I can't do that. I've already said too much."

"Then I guess there's nothing more to say," she said, reaching for her tea.

"No, I guess not," Nat shot back.

They sat in silence, as she angrily assessed him, still hoping they could find a way to break through the latest wall that had appeared between them.

Regretfully, Julianna broke the gaze first to glance down at her watch.

"Oh, I've got to get going soon. Megan's going to be looking for me."

"Yeah, I need to go myself," Nat agreed.

Neither made a move.

"So, is it over between us?" Julianna finally asked.

"Is what over? Doesn't seem like anything even had a chance to get started," Nat snapped. "I've told you I love you and that I want you safe. You've told me nothing except that you don't trust me." He waved his hand to cut her off as she tried to fire back. "No, Julianna, you don't trust my judgment, you don't trust my feelings, and you obviously don't share those feelings. So, no, I guess there isn't anything more to say."

With that, Nat stood to leave.

"Goodbye," he told her, turning to go.

"Oh, yeah, that's right! Just disappear again," Julianna said, jumping to her feet to look him in the eyes. "You have this funny way of always getting in the last word and then vanishing, and I'm tired of it. You say I don't share your feelings? How do you know? You haven't stayed around me long enough to find out. You've never even *asked!*"

She could feel her words echo around the crowded room. As she slowly turned her head, a blush overtaking her face, she realized everyone was watching them with considerable interest.

"And *curtain!*" she said with a sarcastic bow. "End of scene."

Nat just stood there, anger still marking his face, and yet he also seemed entirely unruffled by the matinee they'd just put on.

She didn't care what he or anyone else thought, she decided. *It's my turn to do the disappearing.*

She grabbed her backpack and swept out of the café, happy she'd at least gotten the last word for once.

Too bad half of London had to hear it, she thought as she stalked away.

Chapter 22

Righteous Indignation

JULIANNA'S RIGHTEOUS indignation propelled her for about two city blocks before she started cooling off. By the time she walked another block, however, she was beginning to feel the pangs of regret. By block five she was in a full-fledged panic.

She pulled to a stop, apologizing to the woman behind her when they collided.

"I can't let it end like this," she muttered to herself as she turned around, now fully past the point of caring how many Londoners thought she was insane.

She ran back in the direction of the café, anxiously searching the crowd for Nat's yellow shirt and his black, curly hair. But no luck. Out of breath, she slowed down as she approached the café, afraid of what she'd see— or actually what she *wouldn't* see—through the large front window. Taking in a deep breath, she peered inside.

Nat was gone.

Disappointment surged through her as she turned around and scanned the street on both sides, but he wasn't anywhere to be seen.

I've missed my chance to make up with him.

Rolling her eyes in frustration, she started walking again. Her thoughts were a confused jumble of regret and remnant anger at Nat's audacity. *Maybe I* did *do the right thing*, she thought, picking up her pace.

Glancing at her watch, she realized Megan was

probably worried or, more likely, annoyed. She was late for their scheduled meeting time, and the last thing she wanted was to have one more person angry with her.

Hurrying down the street and rounding a corner, she caught sight of the bookstore in question. Sure enough, an impatient-looking Megan was standing out front, her arms weighed down with shopping bags.

At least someone's having a good day, Julianna told herself as she waved to get her sister's attention.

"Did you forget something?" Megan asked, her irritation apparent.

"I'm so sorry, Meg, but you won't believe what just happened."

"Who got shot this time?" Megan asked.

"No one, but nice guess," Julianna replied. "Nat tracked me down to apologize for what I saw this morning. And, I suppose, to see if I was okay with it."

"Wow, how did he find you?"

"He remembered the itinerary—I showed it to him on the bus."

"Wow. Scary powers of recollection," Megan said. "Okay, so what did you tell him?"

"I said I was fine, but then he morphed into a big macho he-man dictator. He actually *insisted* that you and I fly home right away, and he had the nerve to get mad at me when I refused."

"But Jules, he probably knows something we don't know," Megan said. "Maybe we should think about this for a minute."

"What? You want to give up and crawl home? I don't want that, Meg! Why should we let anyone— including terrorists and super spies—tell us how to lead our lives?" Julianna asked, a hint of a plea obvious in her voice.

"Okay, okay. I just thought he might have said more about the threat he's worried about."

"No, no, of course he wouldn't tell me anything specific. So we're exactly where we were before—just trying to live our lives in dangerous times."

"Yes, okay. I don't want to go back home yet, either," Megan said. "So what happened after you refused to budge and he got mad?"

"We fought. It's all over between us. And trust me when I say it's mutual," Julianna told her. "I can't believe what a jerk he turned out to be."

"Oh yeah, I know what you mean," Megan's sarcastic tone made Julianna laugh way before she reached a punchline. "I can't stand it when gorgeous men try desperately to save my life. What a turnoff."

"Oh, shut up!" Julianna said, her smile staying in place for the first time that afternoon. "Okay, show me what you bought."

Chapter 23

The Setup

BACK IN THE HOTEL a short time later, Julianna walked out of the bathroom feeling soothed. A hot shower had been the perfect way to melt her anger and help her relax.

"Let's see a play tonight," Megan suggested, breaking into her thoughts.

"Oh, yeah, good idea," Julianna said as she headed for the closet. She had packed a great black dress for just such an occasion. "There's a comedy playing that I read a great review of, and it's supposed to be really funny. It's about this guy who—"

"How about *My Fair Lady*?" Megan asked.

"Uh, yeah, okay. That sounds like a pretty 'England' thing to see."

"And let's go someplace fancy for supper," Megan went on, offering up the name of a restaurant she'd read about.

"Yeah, okay," Julianna replied, turning to eye her sister suspiciously. "Why are you suddenly acting like my cruise director?"

"I just wanted to get our minds off today, and this seems like the perfect way. No ulterior motives."

"Mmm-hmm," Julianna said, still suspicious. But she knew Megan could never hide anything from her for long. So Julianna let the subject drop and started getting ready. Megan would 'fess up eventually. And anyway, she was probably right. An evening out would be the perfect way to enjoy herself and to forget a certain annoying spy.

She slid into the dress, then headed into the bathroom to put on her makeup, deciding last-minute to make it darker than usual. If she and Megan were going to have a fancy evening out on the town, she may as well look the part. She finished off this look by putting her hair up in a loose and slightly messy twist and then pulling down a few tendrils to soften the look even further.

Satisfied, she turned to Megan and said, "Hey, whaddya think?" then twirled for effect. "Do I look better than I feel?"

"Oh, yes," Megan said as she slid her own dress over her head, "I'd never know by looking at you that you just broke up with the love of your life today."

"Gee thanks. And he obviously *wasn't* the love of my life," Julianna reminded her, determined to drop the subject. "No more talking about him, no more thinking about him, and especially no more crying over him."

"Yeah, okay, whatever you say," Megan mumbled, stopping to tuck an errant strand of hair back into Julianna's 'do before heading for the closet to pull out the shoes that went with the dress.

"I'm serious, Meg. It's over."

"I heard you."

"Okay, so why does it seem like you're up to something?"

"Gee who's the super sleuth now?" Megan asked, which made Julianna roll her eyes. Was everyone trying to be irritating today?

After Megan finished getting ready, they grabbed their jackets and packs and headed out again.

"Thanks for trying to make me feel better,"

Julianna said, her cheerfulness forced, but her regret over being suspicious of her sister's motives was genuine as they walked through the vacant lobby. She threw an arm around Megan's shoulders and gave her a hug from the side. "I'm sorry I suspected your motives. What could you possibly be up to anyway?"

"Mmm," Megan said, noncommittally.

They walked out the front door and into the cool evening air, accepting the bellman's help in hailing a cab.

*   *   *

They were both quiet on the ride, lost in their own thoughts. Julianna was, naturally, focused on Nat. Despite her earlier bravado, the fight they'd had was weighing heavily on her. She couldn't really imagine that she would never see him again and never have a chance to apologize for walking out on their fight. No way she could live with this weighing on her forever.

The only thing that kept her from completely dissolving into tears was her conviction that she'd been right in her refusal to go back home. He couldn't spend a sum total of ten minutes in her life, and then suddenly expect to take it over.

She was also glad she hadn't blurted out her feelings to him. Those feelings were pretty suspect anyway—how could she love such a tyrant? He was probably thoroughly regretting telling her he loved her. Then again, Julianna was certain that was no longer true, anyway. Feelings that only had a few days to grow could certainly shrivel and die after one big argument.

By the time the cab pulled in front of the restaurant, Julianna was depressed again. She'd been loved by a wonderful man, and that love hadn't lasted the span of a single week. *Will I ever get over him?* she wondered as she got out, sick of her yo-yoing emotions.

They walked inside, and Julianna stepped forward to give their names to the maître d'.

"Hello Tom, it's great to see you again," she heard Megan say behind her. She whipped around, only to find herself face-to-face with Nat.

Then Megan said, "Uh, Jules, I have something to tell you."

"Yes, Benedict?" Julianna answered, locked into Nat's gaze.

"When you were in the shower, Tom called to say hi. I suggested we all get together for the evening," Megan said. "I was afraid you wouldn't come if I told you."

"Good guess," Julianna said, still mesmerized by Nat's beautiful face.

"I didn't know either, if it makes you feel any better," Nat told her.

Feel?!

Julianna didn't know *how* she felt, but she knew she wasn't angry with Megan. In fact, it wasn't anger she was feeling toward Nat at that minute, either. No, that feeling could better be described as lust. He looked amazing. And not just his face, either. She'd never seen anyone wear a blazer so well. It fit perfectly, accentuating his broad shoulders.

"You're so amazingly beautiful tonight, Julianna," Nat said in a weird kind of echo of her own thoughts. He also appeared to be unfazed by the fact that she was practically drooling on him. "I think I forgot to breathe there for a minute."

"Are you saying you need a nurse?" Julianna asked, frustrated she wasn't sophisticated enough to pull off blatant flirting without the usual reddening of her face.

"Yeah, I think I do," Nat said quietly. "I'm so sorry we fought today."

"I'm sorry too, Nat," she said breathlessly. "I was so worried that would be the last time I'd see you, and I would never get the chance to apologize for walking out like that."

"Hey you two," Tom said. "They just called us. Our table's ready."

Nat gently took her hand and led her into the dining area.

Squeezing his in reply, she was happy for once simply to follow him to their table and let him take charge.

Chapter 24

One Tiny Lie

THE RESTAURANT was small and darkly lit, with candles everywhere, which filled the room with an ambience of romance. White cloths covered round tables that were elegantly set with fine china, crystal, and matching napkins. And when Nat held out a chair, it made Julianna feel like a princess.

She gratefully accepted a menu from the waiter, then somewhat absentmindedly picked something that may or may not have contained chicken. After that she agreed numbly with whatever wine and appetizer suggestions were made by the group. She wondered if she'd be able to make an intelligent comment all evening.

"So Megan, what do you do?" Nat asked, picking up his water glass and taking a drink. "Are you a nurse too?"

"No, I can't even seem to get out of college," Megan replied. She looked like she was trying to seem serious, but she was failing miserably as a smirk appeared on her face.

"Oh, don't listen to her," Julianna said with a wave of her hand, happy they'd found a topic she could easily discuss. "She's got her master's of education and now she's working on her doctorate."

"She goes to Rutgers," Tom filled in, reaching for the bread.

"You still live in Paramus?" Nat observed with a

frown. "Bummer of a commute."

"Yeah, but I couldn't leave Julianna in a lurch," Megan said. "You know how rents are around there."

"Whatever you're paying, double and maybe even triple it, and you'll get roughly what we're paying in New York," Tom said with a laugh.

The waiter arrived with their brie appetizer and bottle of wine.

"So how are you two able to have the evening off?" Julianna asked, searching for another safe topic of conversation between bites.

"No one works twenty-four hours a day," Nat said, his tone softer than his words.

"Yeah, we're no help to anyone if we're completely exhausted," Tom said, adding, "which is why I'm going to need to make it an early night."

"You two have had a pretty crazy day, I hear," Megan commented, ignoring Julianna's murderous look.

"Yes, we did, and there's no end in sight," Nat said, turning to look Julianna in the eye. "And I don't want to fight about this again, but have you thought more about what I said? About leaving early?"

Julianna exhaled in exasperation. *Will he ever give up?* she wondered. Finally, she broke the awkward silence that suddenly clouded the mood at the table. "Subtle topic change," she said.

"Yeah, I thought you'd like that," Nat replied with a dazzling smile, clearly trying to charm her.

"Would it mean *that much* to you to hear me say we'll leave?" she blurted out, instantly regretting it as obvious hope lit Nat's face. The charm thing did appear to be working after all, she thought, now completely annoyed with herself.

"Yes! *Please* just trust me on this one and go home," Nat said, reaching for her hand under the table. "Take another vacation at a different time. Maybe we can come back to London someday together."

She raised her eyebrows at that last comment. He was playing dirty now, trying to wave their imaginary future in front of her like a carrot on a stick. Well, two could play that game.

"Fine. We'll go," she said.

Megan whipped around in her chair, surprise and instant fury at her sister's change of heart radiating off her now. "What did you just say?"

"We'll call the airport, I promise," Julianna said, not volunteering more information—or even eye contact—to Megan.

"Okay, let's do it now," Nat said, yanking his cellphone from inside his blazer. "I took the liberty of calling the airport earlier. There's a London Airlines flight to Kennedy first thing tomorrow morning."

"Great, thanks, James Bond," Julianna said, reaching for her wineglass and taking a gulp. *Now what have I done?* she wondered.

After Nat dialed the number—what an amazing memory—he got right through. *How lucky for me,* she thought glumly.

"Yes, we need two seats on the first flight to Kennedy tomorrow," Nat was saying as Julianna took another long drink. "Let me hand the phone over to one of the actual passengers. Just a minute."

He gave the phone to her. She was frustrated with Nat for being so pushy, but then she had played her own part in allowing herself to be pushed into this corner.

Grudgingly, she accepted the phone.

"Hello?" she said. Then an idea came to her—a way out of this mess. She stood and put her hand over the receiver. "Let me take this outside. I'm in a restaurant, and I don't want to give my card information where someone could overhear."

With that, she picked up her bag and walked out to the sidewalk.

"That's the London Airlines Flight 490?" the voice on the other end of the phone was asking.

"Umm, yes," Julianna said, looking over her shoulder for Nat.

Once she was sure he wasn't following her, she flipped the phone shut and leaned back against the wall. She hated lying to him, but then it seemed fairly harmless. He was busy and probably couldn't spend more time with her anyway. Plus, they'd only been there a few days. It didn't seem reasonable to cut her vacation so short.

No, he'll never have to know.... Their fight would be easily resolved, and she'd get to enjoy the rest of the trip—and hopefully the rest of their lives—together.

She closed her eyes, hoping that her list of rational reasoning would help. Even so, she could also feel the guilt start its assault on her.

It's his fault for pushing the issue, she thought, trying to recapture some of her fury from earlier in the day. *He knew I didn't want to go, and he forced me to lie to him.*

She opened her eyes and stared, unseeing, at the moon. She wasn't in the habit of lying, and starting now didn't feel so great. It didn't help that she didn't really believe the propaganda she was trying to bombard herself with. She knew this wasn't Nat's fault. Nat was just being Nat—the gorgeous super spy who was used to being in control of every situation. The wonderful man who was quite obviously only concerned for her safety and welfare.

The man who said he loved her.

She loved him right back. She was as sure of that as she'd ever been of anything. This was right, he was fabulous, and their future together could be perfect.

But her stubborn streak wouldn't let her give in and actually leave early. She couldn't even think about a future in a relationship in which she already felt bullied and controlled. Guilt or no guilt, love or no love, she was staying right where she was. She was going to enjoy this vacation. A tiny lie was a small price to pay for fun and freedom.

She sighed and pushed off the wall, heading back into the restaurant.

Chapter 25

Solidifying the Plan

"IT'S ALL SET?" Nat asked, standing to greet her as she handed his phone back.

"Yep," she replied, and they both sat down again. She refused to look at Megan, whose eyes were boring a hole in the side of her head. "The food's not here yet, huh?"

"No, not yet," Tom said, looking back and forth between the three of them. He was no doubt confused by the tension that had settled over the table like a black cloud.

"Jules, let's go check our makeup," Megan said, getting up.

"Oh, I'm good," Julianna assured her as she faked a fascination with the cold clump of brie on her plate.

"I disagree," Megan insisted. "There's definitely something on you that needs to be fixed."

"Oh, all right...." Julianna tossed her napkin on the table again and looked over at Nat and Tom. "Excuse us, please."

To her credit, Megan managed to contain her anger until they were safely inside the ladies' bathroom, which was empty.

"What is *wrong* with you?" she demanded. "Two minutes with him is as long as you could hold out? What happened to everything you said to me today?"

"Megan—" Julianna started.

"'You want to give up and crawl home?' you said.

'We can't let him tell us how to lead our lives' you said." Megan's mimicky tone was dripping in sarcasm. "What happened to all that? And who's paying for this second set of tickets?"

"There are no tickets—I didn't make the reservation."

"What? You *lied* to him?" Megan hissed. "You *lied* to an agent of the CIA? An officer of the *United States government?!* Brilliant, Jules, really brilliant. You *do realize* that he probably knows how to kill both of us fifty different ways below our kneecaps, don't you? This is just great! What were you thinking?"

"Well, it seemed like a good idea at the time," Julianna replied sheepishly. She felt like a ten-year-old caught stealing candy. "I figured I'd just tell him we'd call the airport. He'd believe what he wanted to believe, and we'd confirm our flights. No one's hurt and no one's lying."

"Then what happened, Einstein?"

"You *saw* what happened, Meggie! He morphed into James Bond, whipped out his spy phone, and called my bluff! What was I supposed to do? Get back into our stalemate from this morning? Actually buy tickets I can't afford or try to go through the hassle of exchanging our seats for an earlier flight? Forget that! I don't want to fight with him—or you—about this anymore, and I definitely *don't* want to go home yet!"

Megan let out a sigh. "So now what?"

"So now we drop it. We'll have a good time tonight, and the next time I see him, we'll be back home. Period. You and I will just go have fun for the next week or so, and he'll never have to find out when our vacation ended precisely. He'll be happy, thinking I'm safe. And that means he'll be able to focus on his job, which will make *him* safe. We're saving his life, really," Julianna finished, and both of them smiled at that last bit of flimsy reasoning.

"You are both evil and psychotic. You know that, right?"

"Just trying to save the world, one CIA agent at a time," Julianna said, grabbing her sister's arm. "Come on, let's go see if our food's there yet."

*   *   *

"Everything okay?" Nat asked, standing up for what seemed like the hundredth time as they returned to the table.

"Mascara smudge," Julianna explained as Megan blurted out, "Lipstick damage," in the same instant. Then they both paused awkwardly until Julianna jumped in with a nervous laugh. "Mascara, lipstick. I'm a mess tonight."

"You look perfect to me," Nat said. "But are you sure everything's okay? You two are acting a little strange."

"It's nothing a night out with our two favorite agents can't fix," Megan said. "Oh, here's our food now...."

They exchanged heated looks of relief over the waiter's arm. *Lying's a lot of work*, Julianna thought, watching Nat from the corner of her eye. She couldn't wait to see him back home, where they could relax and get to know each other over quiet dinners and moonlit strolls. No guns, no hostages, no terrorists, no fights, no lies. It sounded like heaven. She sighed, then realized it came out louder than she'd intended.

"Are you *sure* you're okay?" Nat asked her again, this time in a whisper meant only for her ears.

"Truthfully, Nat, I won't be okay again until both

of us are safely back home."

"Me too, Jersey. And you leaving tomorrow is just the first step. You do that, and I'll be there with you before you know it."

At that moment, it became too much for her. The guilt just *had* to be written all over her face. She smiled in what she was hoping was a convincing way—but then who was she kidding? This man interrogated suspects and read human behavior for a living. And he was quite obviously very good at what he did. Her first-time foray into lies and intrigue was laughable, at best. Yes, her best hope at this point was to just keep her head lowered, shovel the meal down her throat, and steer the conversation away from her imaginary flight tomorrow.

"Are you mad at me because I got you to agree to leave?" Nat asked, his spy powers of intuition kicking in again.

Oh, yeah, I'm well on my way to being a top criminal mind. Absolutely....

What a joke this was. She shot what she intended to be a reassuring smile in Nat's direction, but she was still unable to meet his eyes directly. *Great—more lies.*

"I'm fine Nat. I'm just disappointed in general with how this whole vacation turned out," she said, vaguely aware Megan and Tom seemed to be chatting with no problems. Then again, Megan wasn't the one lying through her teeth.

"I'm not," Nat said, grabbing her hand. "I'm thrilled with how this turned out because it brought us together. Please, Julianna, just look at me."

She braced herself, then slowly lifted her eyes to meet his. She was going to be lost if he asked her directly whether she was lying.

"We'll be together again, I promise. When my assignment here wraps, I'm going straight to Paramus to find you, okay?" Amazingly, he looked like *he* was the guilty party. "I'm sorry I made you cut your trip short. But your safety means more to me than anything. I just couldn't live with myself if anything happened to you."

"Nat, stop, please. Please don't apologize. I know why you did what you did and said what you said. And I'm so sorry, too."

"Why are you sorry?"

"Because...well, I'm sorry we fought. And that we wasted our last day together. And I'm...well, I'm just sorry." She looked down where their hands were joined together on her lap.

"It's our last day together in *London*," he said. "But it's far from our last day together."

"Right," she said. "That's what I meant."

Blessedly, Nat didn't say anything more about it. He just squeezed her hand and smiled. That was better. They weren't fighting, and he seemed happy.

That's the most I can ask for at this point, right? she thought to herself, bringing the wineglass to her lips once more.

Chapter 26

JULIANNA MANAGED to avoid the topic of her flight—and therefore avoid more lies—through the rest of dinner. They paid the bill, then headed to the theater.

The curtain rose promptly at eight. The story of Eliza Doolittle was a favorite of hers, but she found she wasn't able to concentrate on it. Not with Nat sitting next to her, holding her hand.

Though the house lights were out, she could make out the features of his face in the dark. Those beautiful eyes, the wire-rimmed frames that gave him a trendy, studious look when others might just look nerdy. That gorgeous curly black hair. She resisted the urge to reach up and run her fingers through it. He seemed completely caught up in the play, and she didn't want to draw his attention back to her. She didn't need him asking her if anything was wrong again.

Except—*Oops!*—she had stared too long, and now Nat was looking down at her and smiling, a puzzled look on his face.

"Jersey, this isn't the end, you know," he whispered.

"It better not be," she whispered back, her eyes suddenly glistening with unshed tears. She was starting to make *herself* wonder what was wrong. *More of my flawless acting,* she thought ruefully.

He reached over to run his thumb lightly on her

cheek. "Please don't cry, sweetheart."

"I'm trying," she told him with a smile. Then she leaned on his shoulder, letting him put his arm around her.

Why couldn't we have met on a blind date or in line at the grocery store like a normal couple? she wondered, holding back all emotions and forcing herself to focus on the actors. She was in the arms of the man she loved, in one of the most beautiful cities on earth.

What more could she truly ask?

*　　　*　　　*

After the final curtain fell and the applause died down, the lights came on again. She couldn't help yawning at that moment. What a long day—had it only been that morning that she'd been at the Tower of London? That Nat had shot a suspect? That they'd fought afterward? It felt as though she'd known him for a lifetime, yet it hadn't even been a week yet.

They stood and stretched, reaching for their jackets, bags, and playbills.

"Anyone up for dessert or drinks?" Tom asked.

"I think we're going to take a walk, but you two go ahead," Nat told him.

Julianna shrugged at the questioning look Megan gave her. Nat seemed convinced they were leaving. She hoped she could keep his mind on saying goodbye, and she therefore wouldn't have to lie to him anymore. It was true, after all, that they wouldn't be seeing each other for a while.

They walked out of the theater and waved to Megan and Tom, who descended into a tube station and were gone moments later.

Theatergoers crowded the sidewalks as various other plays ended as well, mixing with the tourists and street performers. The sounds of the city surrounded them—the performers' instruments, the laughter of the crowds, the horns of the buses and taxis. But Julianna didn't notice any of it as they walked along, holding hands. All she heard and all she could see was Nat. Beautiful, loving, trusting Nat.

"When do you think you'll be back home?" she asked him.

"I'm not sure. I can't really discuss the details of what we're doing or how long we'll be here. But it could be two weeks or two months. Or longer. I just don't know yet."

"You know, we've never even exchanged numbers or email addresses or anything." She paused to pull a scrap of paper out of her bag along with a pen.

"Well, I can give you my address and number back home," Nat said, taking both in hand. "But I'll have to be the one to contact you while I'm here, okay?"

"More top-secret info?"

"Yeah, something like that. I promise, when this is over and I'm home, you'll be the first to know."

"Okay, but I'm holding you to that. I better not run into you at Starbucks."

"Nope, I'll even call you from the airport if you'd like."

"Deal!" she said with a smile.

"You're a tough negotiator," he teased, making her laugh.

"Oh yeah, real tough."

"You were tough today when we were arguing," he pointed out. "You were strong and stood your ground."

"Oh, please Nat, let's not talk about that anymore. I hate that we spent most of our last day together fighting."

"Deal. See, you *are* tough."

They walked aimlessly for a while, talking about all the things they would do together once Nat came home.

"Oh, I know!" Julianna said, turning her face up to his in excitement. "Let's go to the top of the Empire State Building together! I've always wanted to do that with someone...well, you know, someone who...."

"Who you love?" Nat asked.

"Maybe," she said, a smile flirting across her face. "But what would that have to do with you?"

"Ouch, that was harsh!" he said with a laugh, pulling her into his arms.

"I'm just teasing you," Julianna told him breathlessly, gazing up into the blue eyes she had already come to love so much. *Love....* So was it time to tell him the truth finally? That she loved him just as much as he seemed to love her?

"You don't have to say anything, Jersey," Nat said, once again reading her mind.

"No, no I *want* to," Julianna insisted, but he cut her off again.

"I haven't been saying that to you—that I love you—just to get you to say it back. I want you to wait until you're as certain about your feelings as I am about mine."

"But—" Julianna started to say, then Nat pulled her close and leaned down, capturing her lips in a long, exquisitely slow kiss. She gave in to the amazing feelings coursing through her body as she kissed him hungrily back. She still wasn't used to the electricity that was always crackling whenever they were together, whenever he touched her. It was as astonishing as it had been that first time on the bus. *I could never get tired of this feeling,* she thought, hoping she'd get the chance to prove herself right.

He finally released her, pulling back so he could look at her.

She squirmed a little under the intensity of his gaze, but it was filled with so much tenderness that she gave into it and stared back, trying to memorize his face. She wanted to remember exactly the way he looked at that moment for the rest of her life.

"That's just a promise of what's to come, you know," he said finally.

"Oh, I, uh, don't make it a habit of—"

"You think I won't push you to tell me how you feel about me, but I *will* push you to sleep with me?" Nat asked, running his thumb lightly down the side of her face.

"No, of course not," she said. She knew that about Nat, of course. But there was no way she could sleep with him and lie to him at the same time. She just couldn't do it, and she had to make sure they waited until this mess was over to take their relationship any further.

"We've got the rest of our lives together, Jersey. We're doing this the right way. We're not going to start our future together on a foundation that we rushed too fast to build."

Or that we built with lies, she thought as the glumness rushed back from wherever it had been hiding since the play.

"And I know your feelings about marriage, but we've also got a lifetime to work through that difference of opinion, too," he said.

*   *   *

They reached the lobby of her hotel a short time

later. "Well, I guess it's time to say goodbye, huh?" she said, as regret flooded through her now.

Nat's face was mirroring the sadness she felt. "I guess so."

"Let's just do it fast, like ripping off a bandage," she said, trying to lighten the mood a bit.

"Ahh, fancy nurse-speak, huh?"

"Oh, yeah, sorry. Didn't mean to lose you in my medical jargon."

"Okay, I'll do this your way, but no, you're not losing me," he said, pulling her into his arms again for another soul-shattering kiss. "I love you, honey," he whispered, and with that he was gone, walking briskly out the door and back into the night.

"I love you, too," she said quietly as he disappeared.

Chapter 27

What He Doesn't Know

JULIANNA STAYED fixed to her spot in the lobby for several minutes, staring at the last place she'd seen him. Her thoughts went dreamily from one memory to another. Nat sitting in the dark at the play. Nat kissing her. Nat telling her he loved her. She wished he had stopped trying to anticipate her every thought and need long enough to allow space for her to tell him that she loved him back. *Oh well, like he keeps reminding me, we have a lifetime for that,* she thought as she pulled herself out of the lobby.

She floated—well that's how it felt, anyway—up to her room, hoping Megan was already asleep. But when she opened the door, she was met by the sound of the TV.

"Hey, Meg, I'm back," she said, kicking off her shoes and heading for the bathroom.

"Hey," Megan mumbled from the bedroom. When Julianna emerged from the bathroom in her pajamas— baggy t-shirt and shorts—her sister asked, "So what are we doing tomorrow?"

"Since we missed the British Museum, do you want to do that? I think tomorrow was just a shopping day or something on the original itinerary."

"Sounds good to me," Megan replied. "So did you finally 'fess up to Nat that we're not leaving?"

"No. You didn't tell Tom, did you?"

"No, of course not. This isn't my lie. But why

didn't *you* tell him? I know how you are—I know the guilt must be killing you."

Julianna rehung her dress in the closet. "Guilty as charged, so to speak. But I couldn't face another big argument. We were having such a great time together, and he kept talking about our future and what will happen when he gets back home. I just couldn't break the spell, you know?"

"Yeah, I guess I understand," Megan said. "Still, this doesn't feel like a fully thought-out plan. At the bare minimum, it doesn't seem like *you.*"

Julianna climbed under her blankets. "I know, I know. And you're right that under normal circumstances I'd never lie like this. But, in the end, I still think that what he doesn't know won't hurt him, especially in this case."

Megan turned off the TV and the light, then settled into her own bed.

"Do you think I'm awful for lying to him?" Julianna asked.

"Yes," Megan said, then ducked with a small shriek as a pillow flew past her head.

"I'm serious!" Julianna said, getting back up to retrieve the projectile.

"I don't think Nat had any right to tell us when we could or couldn't go home as long as he wasn't willing to tell us more details of what's going on," Megan said, obviously sorting through her feelings and choosing her words carefully. "But I don't think the only possible response was to invent this lie. Now you'll just feel bad, and it'll always be hanging there in between you two."

"Yeah, you're probably right."

"And Jules?"

"Yeah?"

"Have you given any thought to what's going to happen if we *are* caught up in another terrorist attack? It's already happened twice. I don't suppose three times is completely out of the question. What if he sees us there? What's he going to think?"

"I don't know," Julianna said quietly.

She honestly wasn't sure she knew much of anything just then.

Chapter 28

The Airport Goodbye

THE NEXT MORNING, they got up and took turns in the bathroom getting ready. Julianna threw on a pair of jeans and a sweater, along with a pair of boots made for walking. They were going to be doing a lot of standing at the museum, and she wanted to be comfortable. After Megan finally finished getting ready, too, they picked up their backpacks and jackets and headed for the door.

Julianna opened it and let out a scream. Nat was standing there with one arm raised, looking like he'd been about to knock.

"Oh, sorry to scare you," he said, lowering his arm. "Ready to go? I thought I'd ride with you to the airport."

"Uh, yeah, we were just going to get breakfast first," Julianna stammered.

"It's already seven. Doesn't your flight leave at ten?"

"Oh, yeah, I guess you're right," she said. "We'll just go grab our bags."

She turned around and headed back into the room, ignoring the looks Megan was shooting at her from a seriously annoyed face.

Julianna walked over to her suitcase and snapped it shut, hoping Nat wouldn't see the dresses in the closet or the makeup and brushes all over the bathroom.

"Ready, Meggie?" Julianna asked sweetly, silently

imploring her sister to close both her suitcase and her mouth.

"Whatever," Megan said, shutting the suitcase and then heading for the door.

"Do you want to look around the room one more time for anything you're forgetting?" Nat asked.

"No!" Megan and Julianna barked at him in unison as they pulled the door shut and headed toward the elevator.

"Don't you need to check out?" he asked, fixing a puzzled look on Julianna. He was probably also hurting from the gruff reception he'd received so far, she realized.

"No, we did it over the phone," she said, unhappy she was getting better at lying with practice.

As they trudged through the lobby, Julianna hoped a front desk clerk wouldn't ask them why they were taking their luggage with them a week before their actual departure. But they made it successfully into a cab, where Nat helped the driver load the bags and told him they needed to go to Heathrow.

"You're an idiot," Megan hissed in her ear.

"Oh, just play along," Julianna pleaded. "We've come this far."

"You're still an idiot," Megan said, climbing over their bags and taking one of the jumpseats that faced the back.

Julianna sat opposite Megan's icy stare and waited for Nat. He took the seat next to her and put his hand in hers as they pulled away from the curb.

"I'm sorry for surprising you that way," he said. "I just had a little unexpected free time, and I wanted to see you again."

"It's okay," Julianna replied. "I just hate goodbyes,

and now we're going to have to go through it all over again."

"Sorry, Jersey. You're just irresistible," he said with a smile.

They rode the rest of the way in silence. *Because what else is there to say?* Julianna thought miserably.

Megan was right—she was definitely an idiot.

*   *   *

The cab pulled in front of the London Airlines terminal, and they all got out. The cab driver handed their bags to Nat, who looked like he was ready to join them inside. How far was she going to let this go? She had to get him to leave before he realized they didn't have tickets.

"Please, Nat, wait," she said.

He set the bags down and turned to her. She grabbed his hand and pulled him a few steps away and out of Megan's earshot.

"Nat, I can't do a big tearful goodbye at the gate. I just can't, okay?" she pleaded, the misery clearly showing in her eyes.

"Okay, sweetheart. Don't look so sad, please?" He pulled her into a tight hug. "Thank you for doing this for me—for going home. I love you for it."

"I'm sorry again for the fight. And I'm sorry I didn't tell you everything."

"You mean about your feelings? I told you; we have a lifetime to figure that out," Nat said, leaning down to give her a kiss. "I'll miss you."

He pulled away then, regret obvious on his face, and gave her a rueful smile before he turned and headed back toward the cab. The driver, who had been waiting impatiently, looked relieved that they weren't trying to dodge their fare. He held the door as Nat climbed into the backseat and waved. They continued to stand by the curb and watch as the driver got back in the car and pulled away, blending into the traffic exiting the airport.

"I can't believe you just did that," Megan said quietly.

"I can't believe I did, either. You're right. I *am* an idiot." A few tears made it past Julianna's eyes and down her cheek, and she angrily wiped them away. This was her own fault, so she had no excuse to cry about it.

"Let's go enjoy this train wreck of a vacation starting right now, okay?" she asked.

"Well, when you put it *that* way, sure," Megan said, hailing a cab. "Let's go."

As they endured another ride back to the hotel, Megan added, "You even stiffed him with the cab fare."

Julianna laughed for the first time that day.

"I am *the worst*," she said, and then they were both laughing.

Chapter 29

Shocking News

THEY GOT BACK to the hotel and returned their suitcases to the room. Then they headed for a nearby café to get breakfast, and after that to the tube stop, as they were anxious to get to the museum.

They wandered wordlessly through the exhibits, past the Rosetta Stone and the Elgin Marbles and the countless other bits of antiquity. At first, Julianna could barely focus on anything. But gradually, *very* gradually, she found herself giving in and enjoying the experience. The museum was huge, and soon she was able to surrender herself to it and get lost in the history that surrounded her.

It was late in the afternoon when they finally left. By that time, Julianna was able to forget her guilt, not to mention how much she missed Nat, and just enjoy herself. Days like this were the reason she wanted to stay in London in the first place, after all.

They strolled through the posh streets in search of a place to eat. They wandered for a while but eventually caught a bus to a more touristy neighborhood, where they found a pub and went inside.

"Ahh...." Megan moaned as they found a table and collapsed into the chairs. "It feels incredibly awesome to sit down finally."

"The museum was worth it though, huh?" Julianna said, smiling up at the waitress as she handed them their menus. "I'm so glad we didn't fly home today."

"You were scheduled to fly today? To the United States?" the waitress asked.

"Yes, sort of," Megan answered. "Why?"

"Didn't you hear? A flight to New York crashed today after takeoff. It looks like there were no survivors." Then she added, "I guess you two are pretty lucky," before walking away.

"That's terrible!" Julianna said, feeling her heart start to beat erratically in response to her mounting levels of panic as the further implications of the waitress's words began to hit her. "Oh, no, it can't be. Please, no...."

"I'll go see if I can find a TV showing the news," Megan said. "Jules, don't panic yet. Order me the fish and chips or a burger or whatever. I'll figure out if it was the same flight, okay?"

Julianna nodded as Megan walked away.

*   *   *

Julianna could feel her breathing getting more and more shallow. If she didn't calm herself, she'd either hyperventilate or have a stroke.

Numerous emotions were at war inside her. She was overwhelmed at the thought of so much needless loss. Thoughts about the families affected swarmed her senses and reminded her of the feelings of fear and grief she experienced after 9/11. This time, though, her emotions also included survivor's guilt, which was battling her feelings of relief at the knowledge that she and her sister had been spared.

But she was also in shock about the possibility of that incredible coincidence. What, really, were the odds that *that particular* flight had gone down? There had to be dozens of flights between New York and London, every single day. And there were lots of different airlines, too—British Airlines, Virgin Atlantic, Continental. She focused on breathing deeply as she listed them in her mind. The chances of this crash having occurred on a London Airlines flight—didn't the lady on the phone say Flight 490?—were just so small they were almost zero. Yes, it was ridiculous to even look into it. Plus, it could have been going to either of the international airports that served the New York area—JFK or Newark.

*Still...*she wondered what would happen if it *was* that particular flight. That would mean, well, that would mean Nat thought she was dead. Right now. This minute. Somewhere in London Nat was actually *grieving for her.* Or getting drunk maybe, or even asking himself what her last thoughts had been. He would also likely be blaming *himself* for it. He thought he'd manhandled her onto that flight. He even delivered her to the airport.

She buried her face in her hands. *Please please please please please let this be any other flight in the world,* she thought miserably.

But no, somehow she knew luck wouldn't be on her side here. Look at the way the whole trip had unfolded so far. Of course *it had been that flight. Why wouldn't it be, the way everything else was going?* The crash was probably the big terrorist act Nat had been working to thwart. He was probably freaking out right now, thinking he'd delivered her to the terrorists on a silver platter.

I just couldn't live with myself if anything happened to you....

That's what he'd said the night before. Those words exactly.

She could hear his voice in her mind. *How would he react to this?* she asked herself. He wouldn't actually do anything stupid and drastic, would he? Her heart kept beating its erratic, racing beat, and the panic continued surging through her. She wondered if it was possible to suffocate from a panic attack. She'd never seen such a case, but it definitely felt like her throat was swelling shut. She closed her eyes and focused on her breathing.

"Jules? You okay?" she heard Megan say as she sat down. Before Julianna had a chance to reply, she continued with, "Well, if it was London Airlines Flight 490 that we were supposed to be on this morning, then Nat and Tom think we're dead right now."

Chapter 30

Supper, Sarcasm, and Shock

JULIANNA WISHED, just for a flickering moment, that she had actually boarded that plane. It was the only thing she could imagine that would take away her panic. Her guilt. Her self-loathing.

"Come on, Jules," Megan said. "Open your eyes. You're scaring me."

"What have I done?" Julianna tried to whisper, but the words came out more like a moan.

"Well, for starters, you saved our lives," Megan said. "Julianna, snap out of it! Hey, come on, if we'd listened to Nat and gotten on that plane, we'd be dead. Period. It's like some kind of miracle."

"No, no, you don't understand! He thinks it's his fault that I'm dead! He told me he couldn't live with himself if anything happened to me. That's why he wanted us to leave so desperately. He's going to hate himself. Megan, what if he tries to do something drastic?"

"Oh, come on Juliet, Romeo isn't that dumb," Megan replied. "It could never possibly come to that, not with the resources he has through his job. Don't you suppose the first thing he did was check the passenger list for our names? He's probably back at our hotel right now plotting ways to kill you himself."

"Yeah, great. As comforting as that is, why would he check the passenger list? He knows—or at least he thinks he knows—without a shadow of a doubt that we were on that flight. He delivered us to the airport *himself!* He's not going to torment his soul further by coming to our hotel. We checked out, remember?"

"I don't know. He's in the CIA. They probably were handed a complete passenger list along with their cups of coffee first thing this morning at the official briefing," Megan said.

"Yeah, unless he's so upset he took the day off," Julianna said, putting her face in her hands. "What have I done???"

Megan shook her head. "Okay, fine. You think he doesn't know, so let's call him and tell him. We'll all laugh about it over drinks later. Except, oh yeah, a planeload full of people actually *did* die today! Maybe you can move out of Me-Land long enough to remember that an actual tragedy occurred earlier."

"I don't have his number here," Julianna said, ignoring the end of Megan's lecture. "I don't even know where he's staying. Do you? Did Tom give you any information like that?"

"No, he gave me his home number and email, but he said he never checks them when he's away like this. His family and friends know to just wait until they hear from him."

"That's what I was afraid of. But what if there was a real emergency? Say Tom's Aunt Edna had a heart attack? Isn't there some sort of emergency family hotline or something?"

"Maybe. Even probably. But if you think Tom put me on his emergency hotline list right after Aunt Edna, then you seriously overestimated the intensity of our relationship." Megan said all of this very slowly, as if speaking to a child.

"Okay, yeah. Okay," Julianna babbled, furiously

trying to come up with a Plan B. "Why don't we go to the CIA? Tell them we need to get in touch with him!"

"Oh, sure. Good thinking. Is that 1-800-hi-CIA-one-of-your-agents-has-been-dating-while-undercover-and-first-I-lied-to-him-and-now-I'm-going-to-rat-him-out?" Megan asked.

"Maybe. Let's find a phone," Julianna said, matching the sassy level in Megan's voice. "You're mean and sarcastic in a crisis, you know that?"

"I am when you're being ridiculous," Megan told her. "Why don't we just eat supper? We've sat here so long that they're going to start charging us rent soon."

"I don't think I can eat."

"Well, try. Aren't you the nurse in the family? Don't you know that you getting weak and sick isn't going to help either one of us? Or Nat?"

"Yes, yes, okay. Fine," Julianna said, picking up the menu although she really wasn't able to focus on it.

The waitress wandered back and asked if they were ready to order. Megan got the fish and chips again. Julianna ordered a salad, knowing she wasn't going to eat much of it anyway. Why go through the hassle of making a big decision?

They sat in icy, moody silence while they waited for their food to arrive. When it finally came, Julianna tried eating, but she just wasn't into it. Her stomach was starting to get upset anyway, so she just pushed the plate back and watched Megan eat instead.

"Okay, here's what we'll do," Megan finally said. "Let's go to all the big tourist hotspots and search for him. He told you that's where they were focusing, right? On the places where the tourists go? We found him that way twice, I think we can find him, or Tom at least, that way again."

Julianna just nodded. It wasn't the fastest way to go about things, but she hadn't come up with anything better.

"Tomorrow we'll hit the biggies," Megan went on. "Buckingham Palace, Kensington Palace, Big Ben. Jules, he'll be fine. And we'll find him. Okay?"

Julianna nodded again, unable to look her in the eye. *If I hadn't lied in the first place—if I'd just stood my ground and told Nat no—he might not have been thrilled, but he definitely wouldn't be going through whatever pain he's in now.*

And when it was all over, he wouldn't have hated her, either.

But he definitely will now, she thought.

Chapter 31

Imagining the Future

WHEN THEY RETURNED to the hotel that night, Julianna couldn't help looking around the lobby hopefully, searching for Nat and his beautiful curly hair. Maybe he *had* seen a passenger roster.

This flicker of hope was quickly extinguished, though, as there was no sign of him in the busy lobby. She exhaled loudly and followed Megan to the elevators.

They headed upstairs in grim silence, taking turns in the bathroom and in front of the sink before going straight to bed.

Julianna shut her eyes tight, trying to close out the terrible thoughts that were assaulting her. But it did no good, because they wouldn't stop. What would she do, and how would she feel, if she found out Nat was dead? And dead *because of her?* And because of that, she'd never again be able to look at his amazingly kind, gorgeous, loving face. Never again be held in his strong arms. Never be able to feel that electricity surging through her because of his touch. How would she feel?

Probably about as miserable as she already felt just then.

Because, face it, when Nat finds out I'm alive, he's going to hate me.

It was true—he'd absolutely despise her. She was a liar, and someone as sappy and old-fashioned as Nat would never want to be with a woman who lied right to his face while looking him straight in the eye. He'd never trust her again. Ever.

So all those things she'd feel if he were dead—the loss of his strength, warmth, and his love—those were all things she'd already lost anyway.

The only difference, of course, was she knew he was alive at least. He may eventually hate her and wish she'd died a fiery death in that crash, but at least she knew he was *alive*. And he'd get over her and he'd move on. Someone with as much to offer a woman as Nat would definitely find love again. And he'd be happy. She smiled at that because, at the very least, she *wanted* him to be happy.

And she didn't want to get married anyway, did she? Maybe this whole thing was a much-too-elaborate means to a better end. Sure, they loved each other, but if you didn't share common goals for the future, what hope was there?

She tried to picture that imaginary future that would never be: Nat coming home to New York and finding her, dating her, proposing to her. She tried to imagine their life together—what would it be like to be married to a CIA agent? There had to be significant risks with that, surely. Would they want to bring children into that scenario?

Julianna rolled over, trying to escape those useless, taunting thoughts. Even if she did overcome her fears of marriage one day, she wouldn't be marrying Nat. Because there was no way in this world or the next that he would ever be able to forgive her for what she'd done.

She could hear the clock in the room ticking, and she could tell that Megan was asleep by the calm, even breaths she was exhaling. How could she do it? Despite all that had happened that day, Megan was over there sleeping like a baby.

Of course, *she* wasn't haunted by lies and deceptions. Sure, Tom seemed to like Megan and was probably sad that they'd supposedly died. But Megan would get that cleared up easily and probably be able to take right back up with Tom when all this was over.

Not me, though.

She had to find Nat, admit her lies, and then watch his love turn to hate.

She sighed and rolled over again. She needed her strength for their marathon tourist-attraction spree tomorrow. *Please, God, let me find him tomorrow. I can't go through another day and night like this,* she thought. *And I don't want Nat to suffer anymore.*

No, she just had to find him, face him, and let him know she was alive. Let him off the terrible self-loathing spiral he was surely in at that very moment. Let him yell and freak out at her and call her a million different names if that's what he needed to do. She knew she deserved his anger. She was going to stand there and weather it all, then wish him love and happiness and let him go.

The picture she had painted in her mind of their confrontation was a terrible one, but she knew she had to let it happen.

Because she loved him.

Chapter 32

Splitting Up

JULIANNA SLEPT maybe two hours the entire night.

The rest of the time was spent rolling around restlessly, trying desperately to force herself to go to sleep but finding no escape from her self-recriminations. Her mind bounced relentlessly from topic to topic: how to find Nat, what to tell him, wondering what he was feeling or doing at that moment, and trying to figure out how she would get through the next couple of days. And, finally, wondering how she'd get through the rest of her life carrying the burden that she'd lied to and tormented the only man she'd ever loved.

Yeah, this is going to be a great day, she thought as she finally gave up her struggle around five and just got up.

Megan was still sleeping, so she pulled out her guidebook and spent some time mapping their route. Where should they start first? What sites were close to each other? What sites were the most prominent and therefore the most likely to attract the terrorists'—and the CIA's—attention? Glad for a diversion from her mental rollercoaster of torture, she threw herself into the project.

"How long have you been up?" Megan said a short time later, startling her.

"All night, basically. I'm just planning our route," Julianna said, turning back to the day's itinerary. "Hit the shower, and then we can go get started."

When Megan finally emerged from the bathroom, ready for the day, Julianna took her turn. She didn't bother to put on makeup in spite of the dark circles hanging under her eyes. They stood in particularly stark contrast to the rest of her paler-than-usual face. Then she threw on jeans and a long t-shirt and yanked her hair back in a careless bun tied haphazardly with a scrunchy.

"Trying to convince Nat you actually *did* die?" Megan asked.

"I feel terrible, so I may as well *look* terrible. But thanks," Julianna said, trying to rein in the snappy tone. Absolutely none of this was Megan's fault—no need to take her own lack of sleep and general stupidity out on her sister.

"Well done then," Megan teased, clearly trying to lighten her up a little. "You've achieved 'look like hell' to perfection."

"Hey, we all have our gifts," Julianna replied in an attempt to at least fake being cheerful. "Let's grab breakfast, then we'll start at Kensington Palace and move east through Hyde Park toward Buckingham Palace, okay?"

"Um, okay...." Megan said hesitantly, grabbing her bag and jacket.

*   *   *

The day was gray and rainy, which pretty much suited Julianna fine since it helped her wallow in her funk.

"Okay, let's have it," she said impatiently, stopping in her tracks on the sidewalk in front of their hotel. A tour bus was loading passengers and their suitcases, and thus crowds of sleepy retirees circled around them.

"Have what?" Megan asked, clearly playing dumb as she tried to ignore the tone in her sister's voice.

"You quite obviously think my plan of attack is stupid or flawed or whatever. So let's just have it—what's on your mind?"

Megan sighed and rolled her eyes. "You're not going to like it."

"Spit it out! Meg, I'm too tired and cranky to guess."

"Okay, okay. I think we should split up. I know you want to see Nat and tell him yourself, but if we split up, we'll cover more territory and be more likely to find him."

Julianna thought about this for a few moments. Megan was so obviously right, but she couldn't help but feel that if the truth about her lies didn't come from her, it would only add the final nail in the coffin that contained the dead body of what was once their relationship. *Man I'm getting morbid,* Julianna thought, shaking off this grim mental picture.

"I won't tell him you lied or anything," Megan continued as though laying out her case for the jury. "I'll just say, 'Nat, Julianna's alive. We didn't get on that plane, and we've been scouring London trying to find you to let you know.' That's all I'll say. If he starts asking a bunch of questions, I'll just tell him to come with me to wherever we decide to meet up. Okay?"

"Yes, absolutely, you're one-hundred percent right," Julianna finally said.

"But...?"

"But this, like everything else right now, sucks. It's my own fault, though, and this is what's best for Nat." Julianna sighed. "So I just have to get myself together, that's all."

They walked the rest of the distance to the café in silence. Julianna bought an unidentifiable pastry, then proceeded to play with it while Megan ate, choosing to drink water instead of actually eating.

"Aren't you going to have that?" Megan asked.

"Oh, you know what they say. 'Feed a cold, starve a guilty conscience'," Julianna replied, attempting fake cheerfulness for her sister's sake again.

"As ever, you're a riot. This is all going to be okay, you know. We'll survive this and Nat will too, Jules."

"I know, I know. It's just so awful to think about what I threw away. He's so perfect, and I am such a loser."

"Hey, loser, we don't even know how he's going to react, so stop spiraling," Megan told her. "Who knows? He may be so perfect that he actually has the capacity for forgiveness. He may be so thrilled that you're alive that he'll forget all of this just for the chance to start over."

"You think so?" Julianna asked, hope peeking through the clouds for the first time.

"Honestly, I don't know. But my point is that neither do you. Neither one of us can anticipate what he'll say or do, so assuming the worst and giving yourself an ulcer just doesn't make any sense, any more than assuming the best and ordering wedding invitations would. We just don't know, so let's focus on finding your hot spy, and then we'll both know."

"You think he's hot?" Julianna asked, smiling her first genuine smile in what felt like forever.

"Way to focus," Megan said with a laugh.

"Yeah, yeah, okay. So what's the new plan?"

They got out the maps and guidebooks to once again decide what to do. Julianna, they decided, would start at Harrods, the department store whose green shopping bags were all over London. Harrods was known for its fancy food halls, designer labels, and even some tourist kitsch, and Julianna figured its famous opulence could be a huge tourist—and terrorist—magnet. After trying there, she would go to Kensington Palace and Hyde Park while Megan went to Buckingham Palace and Covent Garden. Then they'd meet at one by the Eros statue at Piccadilly Circus.

Julianna caught a bus to Harrods, but Megan decided the Tube would get her to the palace quicker, so she headed off for the nearest Underground stop.

Please let this work, Julianna prayed as she watched the busy Londoners from her seat on the bus. She let her mind wander to what Megan had said earlier. Was it actually possible? Could Nat, after everything they'd gone through—well, after everything she had put him through—could he actually ever forgive her? Was there even a flicker of hope?

Probably a tiny one, she decided, but no more than that. It was just too much to get past. But despite how small that chance was, how completely infinitesimal it was, it was there. He might possibly one day forgive her.

Maybe.

She clung to that scrap of hope like a life preserver, and for the first time thought she just might be able to survive this mess.

Chapter 33

Searching for Nat

HARRODS was packed.

It was also *huge*. Julianna paused inside the entrance to look over the floor layout that the guard by the door handed her. *You need a map to shop here?!* What *was* this place? And where should she even start looking?

She studied the floor plan while trying to decide what departments held the most allure for tourists. There were gift shops all over the store; one was marked "luxury gifts," another the "Harrods Shop," and then, of course, there was "Harrods World." That one contained a duty-free information area, which seemed to scream *tourist* to her.

She looked for Nat among the souvenirs in Harrods Shop, then got on the Egyptian escalator and went to the next floor, where she wandered through the expansive food halls. Room after room was filled with glass cases of meats, fish, cheese, and salads, most of which were cuts and flavors completely unknown to her. Shelves of spices and sauces ringed the rooms. A visual assault she could only describe as *shellfish art* caught her attention in the middle of one room.

But there was no sign of what she really wanted to see—Nat's face.

She skipped the next two floors—which had tons of departments but whose clothes and linens didn't seem to hold any obvious draw for tourists—and instead headed for the fourth. There she found Harrods

World, Harrods Shop, Planet Harrods, The Georgian Restaurant, The Terrace Bar, and an ice cream parlor. She scanned the crowds while absentmindedly noticing the t-shirts, mugs, kitchen decor, tea and coffee tins, and toys that all proudly proclaimed "Harrods–Knightsbridge." She was taking it all in without really *seeing* any of it. And still no Nat.

After finding the escalator again, she decided to give up on Harrods. She got down to the street level and headed back out into the rain.

Next stop, Kensington Palace.

*   *   *

When she got there, she circled the black and gold iron gates, taking in the splendor of the large brick mansion where Queen Victoria had grown up in the 19th Century and Princess Diana had lived in the 20th. She debated joining the next tour but abandoned the idea since the Harrods stop had taken longer than expected. Plus there didn't seem to be much going on at the palace, and it certainly didn't look like the CIA had set up camp there.

So she headed glumly into Hyde Park, wandering by the lakes, complete with their graceful ducks and swans. The birds, at least, seemed content as they glided through the water, unmoved by the rain.

Julianna smiled at this peaceful scene, although the smile didn't quite reach her eyes. She gave up the attempt at serenity and kept going, noting that the rain made it clear that Nat—and basically everyone else—had avoided the park that day. It was too soggy for mothers and children on the playgrounds or joggers on the paths. The vendors weren't out, either. In fact, given the weather, the park wasn't much of a tourist draw at all.

She started following paths back to the road, where she could catch a bus and head to Piccadilly Circus. She'd be early, but she could at least scan the area. It was basically the theater district, so it would be smarter for them to go back to it at night, but she thought it wouldn't hurt to check it out in the daylight.

When she jumped off the bus, it was only noon. But she could see Megan standing by the golden statue of Eros already. With a mixture of excitement and fear, she scanned the area around her sister. No sign of Nat. Then she finally really looked at Megan, who was just shaking her head in a silent *no*.

The search was far from over.

"I take it you didn't find him, either," Megan said as she got within hearing distance.

"Nope. The park was a complete bust because of the rain. Harrods is weirdly cool and packed with tourists, but not spies. And nothing seemed to be going on at Kensington Palace."

"Ditto for me. Not much happening at Buckingham Palace—I didn't hit it at a changing-of-the-guard moment, for one thing—and no sign of him around the Covent Garden area." Megan then scanned Julianna's face in an obvious attempt to assess how her older sister was handling everything. "Well let's eat. You've got to be starving."

"Would you mind terribly if we just went to McDonalds or KFC or some other place completely American like that?" Julianna asked. "I need comfort food."

"Not a problem," Megan replied, and they headed down the street, finding the familiar golden arches without too much trouble.

"Okay, back to business," Julianna said after they'd

secured their trays of junk food. "Where to this afternoon?"

"Do you think we should retrace some of our steps? Go back to the Tower of London, for example? Or to the British Museum?"

"Yeah, let's retrace a little," Julianna said. "How about you go to the Tower of London and the Tower Bridge, and I'll go to the Victoria and Albert and the Natural History Museums? If I can, I'll go back to the British Museum, although it's not exactly next door to the other two and I don't know how much I can fit in."

"Well, you can't scour every single room of that many museums in an afternoon, obviously," Megan said. "Just check the front steps or plazas, then go inside and look around the ticket areas and gift shops. That ought to do it, don't you think?"

Julianna nodded. "Yeah, you're right. They're too big for me to go through completely. Plus I doubt that's really what Nat would be doing today anyway. Want to meet at the same spot at six or so? We could eat supper, then check out the theaters. We know it's a definite tourist-o-rama around here at night."

"That sounds good, sure."

The plan set, the two finished their lunches, hit the bathroom, then split up again.

"Good luck," Megan called over her shoulder as she headed for her tube line.

"Thanks, you too," Julianna replied. *We're both going to need it,* she silently added.

*   *   *

The museums were definitely where the tourists had decided to escape the gloomy weather, Julianna realized. Each one was packed, so it took her quite a while to survey the crowds. She worked her way through the lobbies, squeezing past the lines and murmuring apologies as she brushed past harried tourists and school groups. The gift shops were just as crowded, making it tough to wander through the racks of postcards and keychains, shelves of t-shirts and mugs, and glass cases of jewelry and silk scarves. And still there was no sign of Nat or Tom or anyone else even vaguely CIA-official looking.

Around a quarter to six, she joined the commuters on a bus and headed back toward Piccadilly Circus, where she found Megan without any trouble. One look at her face, and Julianna knew her luck hadn't been any better. Megan confirmed there had been no sign of Nat at the Tower of London or Tower Bridge.

They ate supper in moody silence, then wandered the theater district, eyeing the crowds lining up for the various shows.

A whole day wasted, Julianna thought sadly, *and I still haven't found him.*

She was starting to wonder if she ever would.

Chapter 34

Spotted

AFTER SPENDING another essentially sleepless night tossing and turning and berating herself, Julianna felt completely defeated the next morning. Megan was trying to stay upbeat and hopeful, but even she was starting to look a little worn down.

"Thank you, Meg, for everything you're doing to help me out of this situation," Julianna said as they walked toward their usual breakfast stop. "I know this has been a miserable vacation for you, and you haven't complained or blamed me or yelled about it once."

"What are little sisters for?" Megan teased, lightly jabbing Julianna in the side with her elbow.

"Yeah, well, you've been really great, and I wanted you to know that I noticed. So thank you. And I love you."

"Well, I love you too, you nut," Megan said. "So where to today?"

"I don't know. We haven't gone to Westminster Abbey, or the Houses of Parliament, or even Big Ben yet. Or the London Eye. How about that lineup?"

"Makes sense, since those are all grouped together. So where should *I* go?"

"Oh, I don't know," Julianna said, pulling open the café door. "Let's just stay together this time. I can't let you miss these big sites because of my mistakes."

"Okay, sure," Megan said, nodding. Julianna noticed and appreciated that once again Megan wasn't taking the opportunity to lay any blame for their disastrous trip on her.

Soon they were headed toward the Westminster section of London. They started at the Abbey, wandering through the expansive cathedral together. They eventually exited and rounded its perimeter, then crossed the street to the Houses of Parliament, amazed at the soaring architecture of the building. They walked down the long side of it, but didn't see many people—tourist, spy, or otherwise—so they didn't bother hunting for a visitor's guide. Then they headed back to Big Ben.

And there was still no sign of Nat.

They crossed the street in silence and walked across Westminster Bridge. Its sidewalk was crowded with tourists and vendors, who were selling Big Ben and Houses of Parliament commemorative plates, key chains, pens, and t-shirts that said things like, "My Wife Went to London and All I Got Was this Lousy T-shirt."

Enjoy the shirt, Julianna grumbled to herself morosely. *All I got was heartache.*

At the far end of the bridge, they descended the stairs that led to the river walkway, then continued to the line of tourists waiting to get on the London Eye. This was a Ferris wheel-type ride with capsules that looked like little observation decks. Megan and Julianna surveyed the crowd. *This would be an obvious place for terrorists to strike,* Julianna thought. *Where are you, Nat...?*

Eventually they boarded their capsule and began the thirty-minute trip around the wheel. Since the historic city lacked the skyscrapers of a metropolis like Manhattan, the Eye offered one of the best views available.

One of the other tourists who was grouped with them had an enormous pair of high-power binoculars, which he seemed happy to pass around the group. Julianna and Megan each took a turn, scanning the crowds walking along the river rather than over the buildings on the horizon like everyone else.

As they reached the three-quarter mark, Julianna got a second turn with the binoculars. This time they were facing Westminster Bridge. She focused in on the walking crowds and slowly let her gaze move from left to right, toward the far end, the side nearest to Big Ben. As she scanned, she caught sight of a navy-blue Yankees cap.

It can't be....

She went back, her heart thrumming as she realized exactly what she was seeing.

Curly black hair shoved under that same Yankees hat, he was also wearing a dark windbreaker and gray sweatpants. Even at a distance, she could see that his face was pale and drawn and covered with unshaven scruff. Seeing him felt like she'd been punched in the stomach. As the pain coursed through her, she suddenly realized she had begun holding her breath. She slowly exhaled again, all the while making sure not to take her eyes off Nat even for a second.

As she watched, he turned his gaze down toward the water of the Thames. Then she gasped as the enormity of the moment caught up to her.

"What?" Megan asked. "Did you find him?"

"Yes. He's there. On the bridge," she said, pointing. He looked as awful as she felt. *Please, please, please don't leave,* she thought, hoping Nat could pick up on her mental plea.

"Probably should give back the binoculars, Jules,"

Megan whispered softly. "You've had them a while."

Julianna nodded, looking once more at Nat's unhappy face, trying desperately to memorize it and wishing just as desperately that she could fly off this sightseeing contraption and down into his arms.

She finally, reluctantly pulled the binoculars from her eyes and silently handed them to Megan, who passed them along to their owner with words of both apology and thanks.

"So we found him," Megan said, turning her attention back to her sister. "That's great news, right?"

"Yeah, but he looks so sad, Meg," Julianna replied as her tears formed. "He looks like he hasn't slept or eaten in days."

"So do you," Megan pointed out. "Just hold on and don't freak out. In a few more minutes we'll be off this thing, and you can go give him the good news."

Julianna nodded. "Yes, yes, you're right." She strapped on her backpack and moved over to position herself by the door. Her plan was to leap off the carnival ride like a gazelle as soon as the doors opened.

Then, on second thought, she took off the backpack and handed it to Megan.

"Can you hold this? I'll be able to move faster if I'm not carrying it."

"No problem."

The seconds crawled by in agonizing slow motion.

"Are they stopping for maintenance?" Julianna asked out loud, sarcasm dripping from each word.

"We're moving. It'll just be another minute," Megan answered in a low, calming voice.

Finally—*finally*—the doors opened. Julianna burst through them like an Olympic track runner who'd just heard the starting pistol, leaving Megan to smile sheepishly at the startled attendant and once again offer apologies on her sister's behalf.

Julianna leapt through the crowd, yelling her own apologies over her shoulder as she pushed past anyone in her path. She reached the river walk and chanced a look to where she'd last seen him.

But he was gone.

"*NOOO,*" Julianna moaned as she pushed herself to pick up speed.

Don't leave. Don't leave. Don't leave.

The words pulsed through her head like a mantra as her shoes pounded the pavement along the river walk. She made it to the stairs, which she attempted to take two at a time. Her general lack of peak fitness combined with her accumulated fatigue, however, was wearing her down quickly. She could feel her lungs start to burn as she turned right off the top of the stairs and headed down the pedestrian sidewalk toward the bridge. Cars and buses zoomed by in the street to her left as she continued to run, though she barely noticed them. Her side was starting to hurt, but she pushed herself forward. Her discomfort was nothing next to the pain she knew Nat was feeling right now.

The sidewalk was packed. *It must be lunchtime,* she thought as she was forced to slow her pace. She kept her eyes toward the railing, always scanning for Nat's Yankees cap. But soon enough she was past the halfway point of the river. He had definitely left the spot where she'd seen him. Had he gone the direction she was heading, toward Big Ben? she wondered. She hoped so as she continued to force her way through the tourists and strolling Londoners.

Finally, she reached the other side, where the vendors had their carts set up. She scanned the area, but there was no sign of him. She looked up and across the street, toward Big Ben, and still he didn't appear to be anywhere.

And then suddenly there he was!

He was down several hundred feet, in a crowd waiting for the next round of city buses.

"NAT!" she screamed in desperation as she ran to the crosswalk. The traffic was flying by; there was no chance for her to cross, and he didn't seem to be hearing her.

"NAT!!!" she cried again as tears blended with her rising hysteria. She'd gotten so close to him. She couldn't miss this chance to see him now.

The light finally turned red, stopping the traffic so the pedestrians could start flowing across.

She screamed his name over and over as she ran to the other side. But a line of the familiar red, double-decker buses, each from a different numbered route, blocked her view.

She made it across the street and started running toward the bus stop. The buses were all pulling away now, and she couldn't tell which one he'd boarded. But he had to be on one of them, because he was definitely gone.

She had found him and lost him all over again.

*   *   *

It was too much. She couldn't take it anymore. The fear, the hysteria, the sadness, the guilt. The pain and the frantic search and the fatigue. She was done. It had all defeated her. She sank down on the sidewalk, leaned against the pole for the traffic light, buried her face in her hands, and sobbed.

She was so tired and miserable and just...beaten. She sat that way, face in her hands, for several minutes.

No one came along to help her…or question her or bother her, either, which didn't really matter since she was beyond caring anyway.

Finally, she heard Megan's voice.

"Jules, come on," she said as she came up behind her. "It'll be okay. We know he's in town still, and we know he's all right. So we just keep searching."

Julianna looked up for the first time and turned her swollen, tear-stained face up to meet Megan's concerned gaze.

"No, no it's all over. We're done doing this. It's like trying to find a needle in a haystack, and we just can't keep it up." Julianna reached for the backpack. "At least *I* can't, and I certainly can't ask you to do it anymore."

Megan held out the backpack and watched Julianna rifle through it until she found her tissues. Then Julianna wiped her eyes and blew her nose.

"Hey, come on Jules. We found him once, so we can find him again," Megan said while offering her hand to help her up. Julianna accepted, then they trudged the few remaining steps to the bus stop.

"No, it's useless. We're wasting our time. We've only got a handful of days left here. I say we use them better. Let's do some actual sightseeing. Isn't that the whole reason I lied to Nat in the first place—so we could stay and enjoy ourselves?"

"Yeah, sure, but that was before, umm….."

"Before we died? Yes, I know. But I just can't take the stress of this anymore."

Their bus pulled up and they got on, ascending the stairs to the upper deck, where they found two seats.

"Okay, so then what do we do about Nat?" Megan asked.

"I'll send him an email. I know he won't get it until he goes home, but at least he'll find out eventually. Then tomorrow we'll go do something fun for a change, and I'll try to put this out of my mind."

"Well, if you're sure," Megan said skeptically. "So what do you want to do tomorrow?"

"I don't know. Maybe just shop or relax or something equally slow-paced. I'm not sure I could take much more than that right now."

"You *do* need rest," Megan replied with a nod. "When is the last time you slept through the night?"

"And maybe we could pick up our itinerary the day after," Julianna went on in spite of Megan's question. "We could go on another bus trip. Take the one to Leeds Castle and Canterbury."

"You're sure a bus trip won't bring back too many painful memories?"

"Everything at this point reminds me of him and has painful memories. But the bus company gave us that free voucher, so we might as well use it."

Megan agreed, although she still looked skeptical.

Julianna didn't blame her. She doubted she'd have any fun, either. But the frantic search for Nat was more than she could bear three days in a row. She needed to find some way of forgetting, or at least of moving forward, and getting their vacation back on track was the only solution that made any sense to her.

How am I going to make it through a lifetime if I can't get through this one day? she thought to herself as she stared out the window.

She leaned her head against the cool glass.

How?

Chapter 36

The Email

THEY MADE their way back to the cyber café near their hotel. Megan agreed to email their parents and create a wonderful tale about how much riotous fun they were having. Julianna, on the other hand, was going to devote herself to crafting the hardest letter she'd ever had to write.

She picked out a terminal that was relatively isolated. Then she laid her backpack on the floor, accessed the right web page, and signed into her account. She opened up a new message window, then pulled out the scrap of paper Nat had written his email address on only a few short days ago.

She stared at his handwriting. He'd used all capital letters, which lent an extra masculine touch to it. Blinking back the memory of the evening they'd swapped contact information, she typed it into the "To" line, then double checked it for typos. The last thing she needed was to write a gut-wrenching opus only to have it bounce back as undeliverable.

She stared for several minutes at the subject line. *Leave it blank? Or maybe try to shove an apology there so he reads it before reading the rest of the letter and learning about my lies?* She sighed and finally decided to just jump in.

She typed in "I'm a" but then her mind went blank. Liar? Jerk? Idiot? Or maybe she should just type "I'm sorry," and let it go. She agonized over it for several minutes before finally adding four letters: L, I,

V, E. "I'm alive." *That cuts to the heart of things,* she thought, satisfied with the subject line at least.

Now for the rest of it.

The beginning was easy—"Dear Nat." But then she lost her momentum. At this rate, they wouldn't make the bus the day after tomorrow.

She sat and thought about the different approaches she could take. Joking? Hard and factual? Pleading for forgiveness? *This is going to be agony,* she thought, staring at the accusing blink of the...insertion point thingy. *What do you call it again?* she thought idly, momentarily mesmerized by its hypnotic flash. *A cursor! Yes, that's it!* She shook off these stupid, time-wasting thoughts and tried to dive back into the letter.

She started—

Yes, it's true. I'm alive. Megan and I didn't get on that plane. But if you've seen a roster of the passengers, then you know that we were never supposed to be on it in the first place. We were never booked on it.

She stopped and reread. This really was absolute torture. Julianna wished again that she'd been able to find him and tell him all of this face to face. That obviously wasn't meant to be, though. She sighed and tried once more to focus. *Now comes the hard part,* she thought.

And if you know we were never booked, then you know something else too: You know I lied to you. I looked you in the eye, and I lied. And because I lied, I'm sure that I destroyed your trust in me, and I destroyed whatever we had growing between us. And because that plane went down, I made you think I was dead.

Nat, it's useless and too little, way too late to say this, but I can't begin to tell you how sorry I am for what I've put you through—how sorry I will be every day, for the rest of my life. I keep trying to picture how I would feel if I thought you were dead, and I just can't imagine it. It's too painful, too absolutely bleak and horrible, and I just can't let my mind go there. So I can't even fathom what I've put you through.

So why did I do it? Why did I lie to you and put into motion all the events that have led us to this point? It sounds so petty now that I can barely stand to write it, but here it is: I didn't want you to tell me what to do. I felt like you were pushing me into a corner that night at the restaurant when you were insisting that we go home. I've been single for thirty years, and I guess I just couldn't stand having to sacrifice even a bit of my independence to anyone, even you. So I faked buying the tickets, thinking that what you didn't know wouldn't hurt you. You'd be able to finish your job with a clear mind, and we'd be able to finish our vacation. And you'd never have to know precisely when it ended, or exactly when we went home.

Clearly I didn't factor in the possibility of that plane going down. I just didn't want to fight with you anymore, and I took the "easy" way out.

Except this hasn't been very easy, has it? Megan and I have spent the last two days searching all over London for you. I don't know where you are, or where you're staying, or how to contact you. So we just searched. I know it sounds like a stupid plan, but guess what? I found you. I was on the London Eye today, and I saw you standing on the bridge. You looked precisely as miserable as I feel. You haven't been sleeping or eating—that much is obvious. And I think you might have been crying, too. I am so sorry Nat. If I ever doubted the depth of your feelings for me, I certainly can't now. I am so, so very sorry.

I got off the Eye and I ran toward you as though my life depended on it. Turns out it did. I missed you by the span of perhaps a few hundred feet. You got on a bus, and there was nothing I could do to stop you. I think I died a little bit as I watched you pull away. I didn't even know which route number you got on to help us narrow our search.

So I guess there's not much left to say. I know you can never forgive this, and I can't even bring myself to ask that of you. So I'll just say this instead: I hope you have a wonderful, amazing life. And I wish you all the love and happiness that you deserve.

Julianna stopped and reread the last sentence before taking a deep breath. This felt so final.

I hope you have a wonderful, amazing life. And I want you to know—even though I guess it doesn't mean a whole lot coming from me right now—that I love you very much. I never got the chance to say it to you in person, and I'm sorry for that, too. But just know that I will always love you.

Please take care of yourself.

All my love forever,

Julianna

She reread everything twice, then stared at the screen without seeing anything. Once she hit the send button, that would be it. The last contact she'd have with Nat. The last time she'd have any excuse or right to ever speak with him again. She continued to stare. *Stupid blinking line,* she thought. Then she took a deep breath and just did it—she hit send and the message was gone, winging its way toward Nat's inbox. When would he read it? And how long would he be tortured by not knowing what had happened in the meantime?

She sighed as she logged off the computer, leaned over to pick up her backpack, and headed to the cashier to pay for the time she'd used.

All those questions didn't matter anymore. It was over.

Chapter 37

Sister Appreciation

THEY STOPPED for sandwiches on the way back to the hotel, then ate in silence as they walked.

As lost as she was in her own misery, Julianna couldn't help feeling even more terrible for Megan. This whole catastrophe wasn't even her fault, but she had still suffered through it all: getting dragged into her stupid lie, making the fake trip to the airport, causing Tom to think she was dead, putting up with her sister's hysterics, hunting all over London in a wild-goose chase for Nat....

And that list didn't even take into account all the fabulous sites they hadn't visited or had been forced to hastily race through. Would either of them ever make it to Stonehenge in their lifetimes? How about Bath? They had lost so many opportunities, either due to the gunmen on the bus or Julianna's mishandling of everything that had happened since. Julianna couldn't imagine how she could ever make it all up to her sister.

Why is Megan even still here with me? Julianna silently wondered as she chewed the tasteless sandwich and plodded along the sidewalk. *Why didn't she abandon this horrible mess a long time ago and strike out on her own vacation?*

Julianna couldn't figure it out. She lost the man she loved, but she definitely had managed to hang onto the world's best sister. She made a mental note to make it all up to her in a big way some day. This whole trip had been *way* above and beyond the call of duty for Megan.

When they got back to their room, Julianna couldn't believe how exhausted she felt. The stress and sleeplessness of the last few days came crashing down on her as she stood in the shower, letting the water wash over her. Numbly, she turned off the faucet and grabbed her towel, mindlessly patting herself dry. She threw on her t-shirt and shorts, brushed her teeth, and turned the bathroom over to Megan.

She was asleep as soon as her head hit the pillow.

*   *   *

"What time is it?" she asked the next morning. *Or is it afternoon?* Megan was up and dressed already, sitting on her bed reading.

"Hi there. I was starting to wonder if you were ever going to wake up," she said, setting her book aside.

"Yeah, sorry about that," Julianna replied, sitting up and stretching with a deep yawn. "Really, what time is it?"

"It's almost eleven."

"Wow! You should have gotten me up a couple hours ago." Julianna threw the sheets back, got up, and padded toward the bathroom.

"Are you kidding? This is the first time you've slept a wink since we died. There was no way I was going to wake you up, even if you had slept all day."

Julianna smiled as she went into the bathroom and closed the door. *Yep, best sister in the world,* she thought.

After she finished getting ready, they headed out for lunch. Neither was especially hungry for anything in particular, so they defaulted to the café where they had been eating breakfast.

"So what do you want to do today?" Megan asked as she dug through her salad.

"Oh no you don't," Julianna replied after sipping

her tea. "This entire trip has ended up being all about me and what I want to do and whose life I'm currently destroying. Today you get to do all the choosing. So the question is what do *you* want to do?"

"Hmm. Well, I don't know. You mentioned shopping yesterday. Other than buying some books in Notting Hill, I haven't bought even one souvenir. Have you?"

"No. All I have is the bracelet Nat bought me that same afternoon. Well, and, you know, a lifetime of regrets."

"Then I definitely think we need some retail therapy," she said, making a face at Julianna's attempt at a joke. "How about Covent Garden? It looked like a fun place, or at least I think it did. I just sort of dashed around it the other day, whenever that was."

"Okay, it's a deal. Covent Garden it is." Julianna stabbed the last forkful of salad into her mouth. "But I'm out of money—pounds, dollars, or any other kind. We've gotta find an ATM machine."

"Okay, good. I'm ready for a relaxing afternoon."

"Yep," Julianna said in an attempt to sound chipper. "Sounds like you picked the perfect diversion. Today I'm going to have fun if it kills me."

"That's the spirit. I can't wait."

Julianna set down her glass. "I've been meaning to tell you again how wonderful you've been through this whole thing. I can't believe how great and how completely supportive you've been, and without even blaming me once for what's happened. We *both* know it's all been my fault."

"Well, duh," Megan said with a smile and a wink.

"All that and you're funny, too. Very impressive. Now, after that heartfelt speech, can you get lunch? Like I said, I'm broke."

Megan pulled her wallet out of her backpack. "You'd be lost without me, you nut."

Julianna nodded with a smile for her sister. This was the most relaxed she'd felt in several days, and she really was determined to make the best of things going forward. *If it kills me....*

They finished up, Megan paid their bill, and then they headed out to find the nearest ATM machine. After that, with money in their wallets again, they found a bus stop and figured out their route.

They were ready to shop.

Chapter 38

Trying to Relax

"HEY, CHECK OUT the bath bombs," Julianna called over her shoulder. They were walking through a bath-and-body shop in the heart of the Covent Garden area.

"Maybe you could stop using the word *bomb* on this vacation, huh?" Megan said, catching up to her.

"Very funny. Seriously, these are just what the doctor ordered. We spend the day shopping, eating, strolling, then I head back to the hotel and take a nice long soak in the tub."

Julianna picked out the rose-scented one, which would leave petals floating in the water after it had fizzed and melted. It sounded nice and decadent to her. She was tired of beating herself up and was ready for a little pampering. Wasn't this trip *supposed* to be about doing something good for herself for a change?

"Actually, you may be onto something," Megan said, her eyes surveying the oils, lotions, and soaps lining the walls. "Maybe this is the perfect place to buy something for Mom, too."

"Oh yeah, good idea. I've got a few coworkers I should bring something back for as well."

They each grabbed shopping baskets and proceeded to load them up with gifts, then met back at the register.

"This was a good idea," Julianna said, smelling one of the soaps she'd picked out.

"And a long, hot bath for you tonight wasn't a bad idea, either," Megan replied. "It's good to see you trying to be calm and relaxed and taking care of yourself again."

"Yep. That's me. Calm. A vision of calmness. From now on I'm going to—" The rest of Julianna's statement was cut off by a woman's shout outside the store.

"Nat!" the woman called.

Julianna froze for a second before meeting Megan's eyes. Megan subtly nodded at her, which seemed to break the spell.

Julianna dropped her basket on the counter and raced out of the shop. *Nat....* Someone was calling for him. She searched up one side of the pedestrian walkway then down the other for any sight of him.

"Nat! *Nat!*" the voice called again. And then—*"Natalie Marie!* Get over here right now!"

Julianna turned around to find a young girl—Natalie, apparently—toddling back to her mother. She watched the mother and child reunion silently for a moment, took a deep breath, then headed back into the shop.

"So?" Megan asked as she finished paying for her purchases.

"It was someone else," Julianna said as she reached for her wallet, her hands shaking as she tried to untie the strings securing the backpack.

"Let me help you with that," Megan said, patiently untying it for her like *she* was the toddler.

Julianna pulled out her wallet and paid the woman at the register, who probably thought she had lost her mind. Only minutes ago, she'd been loudly proclaiming how much calm, peace, and inner bliss she was feeling, but it had to be pretty obvious now that it was all a big lie.

She wasn't calm. She hadn't returned to her old self yet. And she certainly hadn't gotten over what had happened. All someone had to do, apparently, was say the name *Nat* and her emotional house of cards would instantly collapse.

The fun had evaporated out of the day for her. Still, she hadn't forgotten that she wanted to give this day to Megan. She was going to have to force out some cheerfulness for Megan's sake.

"Where to next?" she asked as they walked out, her voice a little too chirpy.

But Megan wasn't buying it. "Hey, really, are you okay?"

"Yes. Well, you know, I got my hopes up there for a minute that we'd found him. But we didn't. Big deal. We still have some shopping to do, right?"

"Yeah, if you're sure?"

"Of course. What am I going to do, mope all day?"

"Well, we *could* keep looking for him if you'd like."

"No, really, it's a wild-goose chase, and we decided to end it. I still think that was the smart decision."

"Okay," Megan said, still not sounding convinced. "If you're sure."

"Yep. Let's go check out the craft booths," Julianna suggested, walking toward the rows of jewelry, hair clips, toys, and other crafts on display in an open-air market. They wandered down the rows, picking through bins, talking to the artisans, and buying a few souvenirs. They spent the rest of the afternoon popping in and out of the various stores that surrounded the plaza, stopping to look at whatever caught their attention.

Once they were completely loaded down with bags, they headed for a table at a pub, grateful for a chance to sit. They ordered sandwiches, then tallied their spending and showed each other their purchases.

After supper, they caught a cab back to the hotel. Neither wanted to fight through the bus crowds with so much to carry.

As soon as they walked into their room, an exhausted Julianna claimed the bathroom first, taking a quick shower before collapsing into bed again.

The pampering relaxation of the rose-petal bath had been completely forgotten.

Chapter 39

Life Lessons

"POP QUIZ."

"Okay, challenge me," Megan said, not taking her eyes off the scenery whizzing by the bus window. They had both been lost in their own thoughts all morning, and Julianna was the first to finally break the silence.

"Recite back to me anything the tour guide has said in the last hour," Julianna said. "Anything."

They had made their last-minute bus reservations without any problems and were now on their way to Leeds Castle, then to the town of Canterbury. The tour guide was an absolute fountain of information about the county of Kent and its inhabitants, possibly going back to the Jurassic Period, but Julianna was finding she just couldn't focus on this rich history, which she would have likely found fun and fascinating under normal circumstances.

"What? Are you kidding? You're going to make me play games and miss what happened to King Whosit of Whatsit in the year eleven-oh-I-forget?"

"Yeah, okay, that's what I thought. Just wanted to make sure my cranium wasn't the only one all these facts were bouncing off," Julianna replied.

"Nah, you're safely stupid with me."

"Thanks. Feeling better now," Julianna said before allowing the silence to settle between them once again. Despite their shopping trip the day before, she was still amazed Megan was speaking to her at all after everything she'd put her through during the last week. So she didn't attempt to analyze her sister's quiet reverie.

Instead, she sank back into her own. Now that she'd faced up to Nat—even though it was only via email—she was attempting to make a mental review of what had happened and what she'd done to make it go so wrong. *Who knows*, she thought to herself, *maybe there's even a life lesson I'm supposed to learn, a reason that I had to go through all of what happened this week.*

A lesson like "don't lie," perhaps? Julianna laughed to herself at the thought. Shouldn't she have learned that one clear back in kindergarten? Was she really that slow to pick up simple bits of conventional wisdom? Apparently she was.

But that was an awfully simple lesson to take away from events that would no doubt change her forever. She didn't like to think things happened randomly, without any reason whatsoever. That was just too depressing. So she was intent on finding something positive or at least beneficial that she could take away from this whole ordeal. Something more than a broken heart, of course.

She thought about it some more. Maybe the lesson was, *Better to have loved and lost, found, lost, found, fought, lied, lost, and found and lost again, than never to have loved at all.* Well, it was possible. She certainly wouldn't have picked *that* lesson up in kindergarten.

She smiled to herself and looked out the window. Fluffy newborn lambs dotted the green fields, making the smile stay on her face a little longer. At least she could still find something to smile about. *That in itself is pretty amazing,* she thought.

She sighed and stared, unseeing, down the aisle

toward the still-chirpy guide, who was pointing out the chalky white land around them, claiming this particular county was famous for it. *Jeopardy, here I come,* she thought.

Her mind wandered once again back to the question of why she'd had to go through the vacation from hell. She remembered back to why she wanted to come in the first place. To get away, obviously. To relax, and to see a country she'd previously only read about. But it had also been more than that—she'd convinced herself that others were leading their lives all around her, while she was sitting still and allowing life to happen *to* her. She'd taken the old saying *Always a bridesmaid* and then she'd run with it until she was *literally always* a bridesmaid. Always planning someone else's future and never living in her own present.

There's the lesson! she realized. *When life hands you lemons, it will also wrap you in yellow taffeta and dress you up like one, then send you to London.*

She laughed out loud, causing Megan to give her a quizzical look. She just smiled and shrugged, and Megan turned away again.

I'm getting a little delirious today.

She backtracked to where she'd been before the lemon-fresh goofiness had overtaken her weary mind—about how she wasn't living her own life. She held that mental image of herself up against the woman she'd been in London. She'd come here and met a fabulous man and let herself fall in love with him. That was pretty daring, right? Sure it was. True, she'd never told him how she felt, but she'd definitely let herself feel it. Those new feelings had transported her from the bitter depths of sadness and remorse to giddy and amazing heights of emotional intensity she never imagined she could feel. That didn't sound like a woman who was hiding and not really living, right?

Right...?

And what about her fear of marriage? What if Nat appeared before her right this minute, got on one knee, and asked her to spend the rest of her life with him?

She'd probably have to sign her soul over to the devil for all eternity, since the chances of that happening *without* a bargain with the devil rivaled the chance of her being named the next Queen of England.

Okay, so aside from that minor detail, what would I do?

As torturous as it was, she let her mind wander in that imaginary direction—marrying Nat, buying a home together, having little curly-headed babies with blue eyes, and living out all the other details of Nat's sappy dream.

Sounded pretty wonderful, quite honestly. And not scary at all.

She sat up straighter, shocked at how completely wonderful that vision really was.

Maybe she'd been wrong. Maybe her insistence that she would never submit to the traditions of a wedding and a subsequent marriage was nothing more than a coverup for her fears. Fears that she'd never find someone worth going through all of that with. Or fears that her current life of hanging with her friends and family all the time would have to come to an end, and she'd be forced to grow up.

So if all that was true...then her trip to London demonstrated that it *was* time to grow up and let herself fall in love and move forward.

Which was a pretty great lesson....

She just wished it hadn't been such a painful thing to learn. How could she ever move forward if she couldn't forgive herself for this debacle or forget about Nat?

Life lessons suck, she thought with a sigh.

Chapter 40

The Hedge Maze

"YOU ALMOST let us leave England without seeing the dog-collar museum?!" Megan whispered to Julianna as the tour guide spoke to the group. "That's the last time I put you in charge of the itinerary."

They were standing on the grounds of Leeds Castle, a fortress built on an island, making it a safe haven for its owners back when raids on castles were something to worry about. It was now a tourist destination known for its beautiful grounds and gardens, aviary, and hedge maze, as well as for its meticulously preserved interior. And, of course, for its dog-collar museum.

"I got you here, didn't I?" Julianna replied.

The guide was encouraging the group to follow her around the perimeter of the castle to reach the tour entrance. They dutifully followed the crowd, which was stopping frequently for pictures of the ivy walls, the swans on the lake, and the daffodil-covered hills that lay on the other side of the water.

"So tell me the truth, how're you doing today with this bus trip?" Megan asked. "Too many memories?"

"The hardest part was getting *on* the bus this morning," Julianna admitted as they stopped so a couple in front of them could finish taking pictures of each other. "I kept scanning the passengers hoping I'd see him."

"Yeah," Megan said as they started walking again.

"I was hoping the same thing, for your sake."

"Would have been perfect, huh? We met on a bus. We might as well break up on a bus." Julianna rolled her eyes.

"Nothing says romantic closure like transportation coincidences."

"Gee, thanks for understanding," Julianna said as they finally caught up with the rest of the group.

The tour of the castle managed to divert her attention from her bleak mood to some degree. The old home was undeniably beautiful, and the period clothing and furniture displayed in the rooms added to the castle's magical presence, making her feel as though she had stepped back in time. They went slowly from room to room, asking questions of the many guards, or docents, or whoever they were.

"So the castle is still in use as more than a museum?" Megan asked one of them.

"Oh, yes. We've had everyone from local charity organizations to United States presidents stay here," the guard offered proudly.

"So it can be used for official functions? That's interesting. But could *anyone* rent the facilities, say for a wedding or something?" another tourist asked.

"Of course. We've had many weddings take place here," the guard said with a smile. "Are you planning one?"

"No, no. Just curious."

Weddings...great, Julianna thought sourly. Her gloomy mood, she found, hadn't really gone anywhere. It had just been taking a bit of a break, waiting for the vision of a wedding—and the realization that she'd certainly never get to have one with the man of her dreams—to assault her.

She wondered idly if the guards would tackle her and throw her into the moat if she gave Megan a good kick for starting the questions that had led up to that subject. She tried smiling at the mental image, but her face seemed to just contort into a painful grimace instead.

Getting over Nat is going to be a very, very long process, she finally admitted to herself as they wandered into the next room.

*   *   *

By the time the tour was over, and they found the exit door, Julianna had made yet another promise to herself to enjoy the day or die trying. She was sick of being miserable, and this was as good a time as any to exorcise the ghosts of her doomed relationship.

"I'm glad we came," Julianna said as they started walking around the grounds. "I really needed this."

"Yeah, me too. I'm glad we're trying to have at least one normal day of vacation."

They kept on wandering, following signs to the aviary and the hedge maze. The path took them through a little courtyard where tourists could sit and sip tea or eat ice cream during the warmer months. Then the path continued through a garden where a young man in jeans was busily planting new flowers.

"This place is gorgeous," Megan said. "Wanna go into the aviary?" she asked as they approached the entrance to it.

"Nah. Getting lost in shrubbery is more my speed today," Julianna said, looking to the hedge maze. "Call for help if you don't see me in thirty minutes."

"No problem," Megan said as she made her way toward the birds.

Julianna continued her solitary walk to the maze entrance. She didn't see anyone around, and she thought it was a good thing Megan knew she was entering the maze alone. Having her body found in a maze weeks later would pretty much be in keeping with the way the vacation was going. Still, some time alone wouldn't be a bad thing.

The maze had a stone lookout platform in its center. Evidently the goal of entering the maze was to reach that platform, see the view, and mock the other rats still stuck in the maze.

"Here goes nothing," she muttered to herself as she went through the entrance and began making choices as to which paths to take. With every dead end, she would reverse herself, trying to keep track of which paths she'd already tried. No matter how intently she focused on it, however, she soon became hopelessly lost. But she could always see the platform above the walls of shrubbery, so she tried making choices that seemed to send her closer to the middle. When she finally reached the perimeter of the platform, she went to the left to try to find the staircase. That, too, brought her to yet another dead end.

She turned right to see if the entrance was in the other direction.

Nope, just another dead end.

She'd approached it from the wrong side, apparently. As she stood wondering in frustration what her next move should be, she heard footsteps. It sounded like someone else in the maze—someone who had managed to find the stairs.

She backed up as far as the hedge behind her would allow and strained to catch a glimpse of the maze conqueror. Maybe he or she could give her some tips.

As she stood gazing up, a face came into view over the side.

She gasped.

Chapter 41

Seeing a Ghost

She couldn't help the small gasp that escaped her mouth as she gazed at his precious face. The moment stretched out between them, and she was struck by a feeling of grateful wonder. All that searching that they'd done! All the planning and plotting and agonizing to find tourist destinations and cover the whole city, when apparently they'd been going about things the wrong way the entire time. All she'd needed to do was wander around and get hopelessly lost in some shrubbery.

"Jersey?" Nat whispered, blinking his eyes as though he'd seen a ghost.

Well, to be fair, he is seeing a ghost, Julianna thought nervously. At least as far as he knew.

"Yes—I'm alive."

It was all she could think to say, recalling the subject line from her email to him. Seeing his startlingly handsome face again, Julianna was once more mesmerized by his eyes and the electrified energy coursing through her body. He was here! She'd finally found him! Offering up more words or explanations just didn't seem possible in that moment.

Nat seemed to be trying in vain to say something, but his shock was clearly overwhelming him, too. She only heard a whisper as his mouth formed a breathless, "Oh." Then his senses returned to him, and tears started flowing down his face.

Before she could react, he put one hand on the platform and used it to propel the weight of his body over the walls of the tower. He landed neatly in front of her.

"Wow," she said.

Nat looked at her closely, his eyes scanning every feature. He seemed desperate to memorize every detail of her appearance, even as Julianna was forced to witness the agony etched on his haggard face.

He finally reached for her, and she flung herself into his embrace. They held each other tightly as Nat's body shook with sobs, and the pain of the last several days crashed around both of them. Julianna held onto him as closely as she could, her own tears forming a pool in the crook of his neck and her mascara staining the shoulder of his shirt.

Neither spoke, but words couldn't have captured the depth of Julianna's emotions anyway. All she knew was that she had to hold onto him, so she clung around his neck as his body slowly stopped trembling and his sobs turned to ragged gasps.

"How...." Nat finally whispered in her ear. "How have I been given this second chance to hold you?"

"Nat," Julianna said with a regretful sniff and a shake of the head. Then she gave him one more hug, knowing it would probably be the last, before pulling away reluctantly.

She ran a finger gently down his tear-lined face, knowing his look of love would soon dissolve into hatred. But she couldn't delay the inevitable any longer. It wasn't right and it wasn't fair. It was time to tell him everything. She wouldn't be admitting her own stupid guilt via an impersonal email after all. She was going to get the chance to tell him in person.

She had known all along that this moment would be hard. She just hadn't really fathomed *how* hard. And how excruciatingly gut-wrenching his grief would be.

She turned her gaze up to his. It was time.

He deserved to know the truth.

Chapter 42

The Truth

"NAT, I AM SO, so, so very sorry," she said, her tears flowing again.

"What?" he said, incredulity showing in his face as he started to say more, but Julianna rushed to stop him. This was hard enough.

"Please, I promise I'll answer your questions, but just let me get this out. This is the hardest thing I've ever had to say, so I just need to do it, okay?"

"Uh, okay," Nat said. "Sure." He then used his thumb to wipe away the dark tracks of makeup her tears had left on her face.

She grabbed his hand with both of hers to stop him. This was all too painful and bittersweet. Here he was trying to comfort her mere seconds before his love would turn to bitter hatred. She held his hand a moment more, then released it and took a step back.

"Please, I can't touch you. And trust me, you won't *want* me to touch you when I'm done explaining."

"That's impossible," Nat said, stepping toward her to close the space between them once more. "Wait, are you breaking up with me? Is that what's happening?"

"What? No!" Julianna said. This was not going at all the way she imagined it might, and she'd conjured up some incredibly painful scenarios. Actually having this conversation, though, was much, much worse than any of them. "Nat, please, just stop and listen to me. I'm begging you."

Something in her grief-ravaged tone reached him, because he froze and looked at her questioningly. Finally, he dropped his arm back to his side.

"Okay, I'm listening, sweetheart. Go ahead."

"The thing is, all of this is my fault. I lied to you, and I'm so sorry."

He looked completely confused as he stood there mutely, watching her struggle to find each word.

"And I'm sorry for all of *this*, too," she went on, gesturing back-and-forth between the two of them. "This is so much harder than I thought it would be."

"I guess I still don't understand," he said. "What is?"

"Telling you the truth and watching your love for me turn into hatred."

Julianna paused then to study his face, trying desperately to burn the image into her memory.

"Oh, come on, that's not going to happen," Nat said, raising his hand halfway, then awkwardly dropping it back at his side again.

Nicely done, Julianna thought to herself, *you're really making this hard on him.*

"Yes," she said slowly, "it *is* going to happen. That night in the restaurant, on the day we fought about Megan and me leaving, I felt backed into a corner. I felt like you were pushing me around or trying to take away my independence or whatever, so I lied to you just to put the argument behind us without having to concede anything. And so I could get my own way, which of course I can see now was very childish."

The light of understanding flickered in his eyes. "You never bought those tickets, did you?" he asked.

"No, I didn't. We were never booked on that flight."

"But I went with you to the airport!" he said, his tone a mixture of disbelief and the first traces of anger.

"That's right. You caught Megan and me heading out the door to spend the day at the British Museum. I was so shocked that you actually showed up, I just choked. I'd gone so far with the lie, it seemed harmless to take it a little further. I figured what you didn't know wouldn't hurt you. And maybe it would even help you. Because then you'd be able to concentrate on your job if you thought I was gone, and I'd be free to do what I wanted to do."

"Worked like a charm," he said, his words now caustic and pointed.

"Obviously I never dreamed the plane would go down. I thought I really *would* die when we heard about it that night. I had no way of finding you! I didn't know how to get the message to you that I was okay." The sobs and the gasping were back. Julianna tried to force herself to calm down, as Nat just stood staring at her angrily. His need to comfort her was obviously gone.

"I am so sorry!" she sobbed, as Nat stepped closer to her, his stony gaze boring its way into her soul.

"Well, that just makes it all better, doesn't it? Do you have any idea at all what you just put me through? Any guess as to how much agony I've been experiencing? I thought I'd *killed* you! I thought that, through my arrogance and insistence that I knew what was best, I had murdered the only woman I ever loved! There is no way in the world you could ever grasp what my pain has been like. But you've been okay, haven't you?" This came out more like a statement than a question. "Here you are, happily vacationing, while I've been counting the seconds until I might be able to join you."

"No, Nat, no! That's not how it's been!" she cried, reaching for his hands and clasping them tightly in her own. "I didn't know how to reach you, so Megan and I spent the last couple days searching all over London for you. We went to all the tourist spots, thinking you were still working to find the terrorists."

"Great plan."

"We knew it was a longshot, but it's all we could come up with! And it worked, by the way! I found you two days ago! We were on the London Eye, and I spotted you standing on the bridge. Oh, Nat, you looked so sad! I was stuck on the ride so I couldn't reach you. When we got off, I ran to the spot where you'd been, but you had left already and then I saw you getting ready to board a bus."

"Wait, you were calling for me, weren't you?"

"You heard me?"

"Yes. I thought I was losing my mind," Nat said, shaking his head at the memory. "So I just climbed on the first bus that pulled up to try to escape that pain."

"Well, then that's just one more thing I have to apologize for. I know you can never forgive me for any of this, Nat, I really do. I know I put you through so much agony that you'll hate me for the rest of your life." Julianna couldn't help noticing that he wasn't contradicting any of this. But then what did she really expect? It was certainly what she deserved.

She took a deep breath and continued, "I'm also so very sorry that I never said this before, but I wanted to tell you how much I truly and deeply lo—"

"Don't say it!" Nat snapped, the force of his words startling her. She dropped his hands and watched as the anger darkened his face. "Don't you dare even *try* to lie to me again."

"It's not a lie, though! I know how I feel, and—"

"Stop it! I don't want to hear it! Please just give me the dignity of hearing those words for the first time one day in the future, hopefully from a woman who doesn't lie to me and make me believe she's dead."

"Nat, I'm so sorry!" Julianna said as she again reached for him.

"No. *Don't.* I don't want to hear any more! Don't contact me! Don't even *think* about me!"

He stepped backward, out of her reach and toward the path that led back into the maze. He stopped for just a moment, his gaze still on her face. Their eyes locked, and Julianna thought for one heartbreaking moment that he just might soften toward her again.

"Nat...." she began.

"Have a nice life, Julianna," he said, then he turned and headed back into the maze.

"Wait!" she yelled, then she tried to run after him.

But he was already gone.

Chapter 43

Reeling and Hurting

"JULES! HELLO?" Megan called out. "We're going to miss the bus. Where are you?"

"Over here," Julianna said listlessly, waving her arm over her head.

"I found a guard who works here. He's coming in after you."

"Thanks. I'm over here," she said again.

"I see you, ma'am," the man's crisp British accent wafted through the hedge comfortingly. "Be right there!"

She'd spent the last several minutes wandering around in the maze, hoping she'd run into Nat again. She just wanted to look at him, and apologize, one more time. But he'd obviously CIA'd his way directly out of the maze without a single wrong turn. Her instincts were clearly not as honed.

"Okay, there you are," the elderly man said cheerfully, pretending not to notice her puffy, tear-stained face. "You got yourself quite lost, now didn't you?"

"Yes, I really did. Thank you so much for the rescue," she said, grateful for his friendly smile.

"This way then," he replied, turning to lead her back. "Your sister tells me you've only got another fifteen minutes to catch your tour bus."

"Yes, thank you. I'd definitely miss the bus without your help."

She followed closely at his heels, amazed at his obvious comfort and expertise in navigating all these confusing pathways.

"Jules, you okay?" Megan asked, taking in Julianna's bedraggled state as they emerged minutes later. Julianna thanked the guard once more before turning back to her sister.

"Other than being hopelessly lost in the maze and reenacting scenes from *The Shining?* Yeah, I'm great. And guess who I ran into?"

"Jack Nicholson? Jack the Ripper? William the Conqueror? Prince William?"

"Great guesses, but no, I ran into Nat. I finally got a chance to tell him the truth."

"Wow, what's he doing here?"

"Took a bus trip, just like us, I guess," she said. "Speaking of buses, we better go find ours."

"So he didn't take the news too well, huh?"

"At first he was so shocked and so happy to see me. He just held me and cried," Julianna said, wiping her eyes at the memory. *How can I possibly have more tears in me?* she wondered.

"But then you told him the truth," Megan guessed with predictable accuracy, "and he reacted exactly the way you thought he would, right?"

"Yes," Julianna whispered. "He hates me and told me not to contact him or even think about him again. He didn't want to hear me tell him I love him, either."

"Oh Jules, I'm so sorry! I was hoping, for your sake, that he'd be willing to just forget everything."

"Yeah, despite everything I've said, I guess that was what I was secretly counting on, too. It just hurt so much to hear him say those things and watch him leave, knowing I'd never see him again."

"But at least now he knows you're alive," Megan pointed out. "You can stop worrying about that."

"Yes, you're right. Despite everything, I'm grateful I got the chance to tell him to his face. He obviously deserved that much. Now he can move on with his life."

"And so can you," Megan said, gently putting her arm around her sister's shoulders and giving her a sideways squeeze.

"Thanks, Meggie."

*   *   *

The rest of their hike to the bus was made in silence. Julianna was too devastated to vocalize what she was feeling, even to her sister.

"And there you two are!" their tour guide said, greeting them cheerfully before following them into the bus to do one last head count. "I think we've got everyone now."

Megan and Julianna headed back to their row and sat down. Julianna leaned her forehead against the cool glass of the window and stared out blankly as they pulled away from the castle grounds. She found she couldn't help scanning the other bus groups, looking for Nat, but she didn't see him anywhere.

She sighed and leaned back in her seat, closing her eyes. She tried to surrender herself to a nap, but the awful scene that had just played itself out in the hedge maze kept looping over and over in her mind.

Nat sobbing. Nat holding me. Nat's loving gaze slowly turning hard and icy. Nat telling me he never wants to see me again. She didn't know how she'd ever get those painful images out of her head.

The tour guide's history lesson, which cut through Julianna's depressed haze, turned to tales of Canterbury.

The town was famous for, among other things, the murder of Saint Thomas à Becket, who was killed at the cathedral. Pilgrims had been flowing into the town since then, coming to visit his grave, though the man's remains had been dug up and destroyed after a decree by King Henry the Eighth.

The macabre tale fit nicely with Julianna's mood, and she decided it was an appropriate destination for her, considering the grim emotional drama she'd just endured.

Maybe Nat will be there, too, she couldn't help thinking. She knew he said he didn't want to see her again, but maybe he'd had the chance to think about it and reconsider. Maybe by the time she caught up with him, he'd be ready to talk some more.

A small flicker of hope eclipsed her depression for a fleeting moment, but then she angrily crushed it out. *Yes, he'll get past all of what happened in an hour or so. Sure. Keep dreaming.*

He was out of her life for good. The sooner she accepted that—and really, truly believed it—the better off she'd be.

Maybe one day it would even stop hurting so much.

Chapter 44

Lunch and Longing

THE BUS pulled into the quaint little town just in time for lunch. The guide offered to recommend a spot, or they could choose to find one on their own.

"I can't bear to sit and play nice, happily swapping, 'So where are you from?' stories with everyone," Julianna said to Megan. "Not today."

"No, of course not," Megan agreed. "I think it'd be more fun to find our own place for lunch anyway."

They got off the bus with the others, lingering just long enough to note the time and place they were supposed to meet later that afternoon.

When the plans were set, they headed off down one of the main tourist streets, an adorable little avenue lined with stores that appeared charmingly ancient but were unfortunately filled with familiar American wares.

"We could be in a mall in Paramus," Julianna complained.

"Yeah, where are the cute local shops filled with cute local crafts?"

They continued wandering and eventually found some with a more local flavor, including a gift shop for the cathedral and a store filled with beautiful ceramics that was appropriately named *Canterbury Pottery*.

"Now this is more like it," Megan said, peering inside. "Let's check it out."

After loading up on pottery that included coffee mugs and Christmas ornaments, they found a restaurant and ordered sandwiches and soup.

"So I know you probably don't want to talk about him," Megan began, "but I'm honestly curious about why Nat was on that bus trip today."

"You don't think he was just trying to take a day off and attempt to forget about his dead girlfriend?"

"Honestly, no. Why did he take the *first* bus trip? Because he's tracking terrorist activity. And since no one's sure what really caused the plane crash yet, I think it's reasonable to think he had extra motivation to hunt these guys down after our supposed deaths."

"So you're thinking we may be right back where we started—in the middle of a terrorist plot against tourists?"

Megan paused, considering this while chewing. "Yes, I guess that's exactly what I think."

Julianna sighed and rolled her eyes. "Can we pick a great time to go on vacation or what?"

"Yep. We should open a travel agency as soon as we get home and bring this kind of joy to others."

Julianna stared at her half-eaten sandwich, then turned to look out the front window of the restaurant at the passing tourists.

"I hope Nat doesn't get hurt. He was so upset after I told him...well, what I told him. I hope he's able to concentrate on what he's actually supposed to be doing."

"Sure he will, Jules. He's a professional. And I'm sure Tom's got his back covered either way."

Julianna nodded, hoping this was right. She couldn't stand to be the cause of him getting hurt—or worse—because he was distracted and upset.

"Are you done there?" Megan asked, cutting into these grim thoughts. "We'd better get moving if we want to see the cathedral."

"Yeah, I'm done."

They cleared the trash off their table and headed for the door. Then they walked out into the bright sunlight—the first they'd seen in days—and joined the other tourists on the street. Unable to help herself, Julianna scanned the crowd for Nat, but she didn't see him anywhere. More depressed than ever, she silently followed her sister across the street toward the elaborately decorated archway that welcomed visitors into the cathedral's courtyard.

Tour groups were standing in huddled circles, listening to guides explain the history of the church and point out the site where its famous Christian martyr had been murdered.

As they stopped to listen, Julianna felt an odd, tingling sensation, as though she were being watched. She turned around.

And there he was.

*　　*　　*

Standing across the courtyard, about to enter the cathedral, was Nat. His face didn't look particularly angry anymore, but it didn't exactly light up with love and excitement, either. She couldn't move, and she certainly couldn't look away. So she just stared back.

"Jules, what is it?" Megan asked, looking with concern at Julianna's face. She turned her head to follow Julianna's line of sight. "Oh wow, he's here. Okay, well, why don't you go talk to him?"

Julianna couldn't reply and still couldn't move. All her senses beyond sight seemed to have abandoned her. And what an amazing sight he was! Despite all that had happened and all the unhappiness and anger that now existed between them, she still felt the familiar leap of excitement that she always experienced when Nat was near. *Things could have been so great,* she thought as a fresh wave of sadness washed over her.

She shook this thought away and took one tentative step toward him while raising her hand to form the "I love you" sign. But Nat didn't acknowledge he'd gotten the message, and her movement was apparently all it took to break the hypnotic spell between them. He turned around and headed into the cathedral instead.

Julianna stopped.

"Oh, Jules. I'm so sorry," Megan said.

"See? He hates me."

"No. That look he was giving you wasn't hatred. He was as captivated by the sight of you as you were by the sight of him."

"So why'd he just walk away?"

"He's not ready yet, Jules. Just give him time. He'll come back to you one day, I'm sure of it."

"Meg don't," Julianna begged, finally taking her eyes off the spot where she'd last seen him. "Don't give me false hope. It's better to just accept that it's over. It hurts more now, but it'll help me get past this in the future. Like maybe when I'm a hundred."

"That's the spirit!" Megan said with a weak smile.

Julianna smiled back, although it felt more like a grimace. That was something else she needed to work on in the next seventy years. Forgetting about Nat and learning how to smile again.

She had her work cut out for her.

Chapter 45

A Bucket of Trouble

SHE COULDN'T HELP herself—she had to follow him inside.

Moments later she was surrounded by sweeping columns and elaborate stained glass and intricate carvings and hundreds of years of tradition, yet all she could do was scan for Nat. She and Megan made their way around the interior and then went behind the altar. Megan was taking in the small chapels that lined the circumference of the church, but Julianna saw none of it.

"Wow, look at this!" she heard Megan exclaim behind her.

"Mmm-hmm," Julianna mumbled, still trying to spot Nat's familiar dark curls.

"Yes, I can tell you're inspired."

Julianna whispered an apology but kept walking. There weren't really that many other people near them, she noted. Those tourists must have started their exploration of the cathedral in the crypt below. *Maybe that's where Nat is right now.*

That thought made her pick up her pace.

She rounded the side of the altar, then slowed as she caught movement out of the corner of her eye. There, in a roped-off area, was a candle burning on the floor. It was marking the spot where Becket's remains had once been buried. Julianna remembered this from their guide's explanation. But it wasn't the candle that made her stop. It was the man standing in the roped-off area.

He was dressed in a gray jumpsuit, like something a mechanic or an old gas-station attendant would have worn. He held a mop and had a large, plastic bucket on wheels. *A janitor, obviously,* Julianna thought. But she couldn't take her eyes off the man's face.

He was so familiar. Where had she seen that face before? She knew without a doubt she knew him. But why? Why did she feel the need to keep herself hidden from him in the shadows of the old church? And where would she have previously run into a creepy Canterbury Cathedral employee?

Maybe earlier today? In the pottery shop, perhaps? No, she quickly was able to dismiss that guess. They'd been helped by a woman clerk and had been the only customers.

At the restaurant? She mentally reviewed their lunch and tried to remember what the cashier had looked like. *Had she noticed any of the other diners?* No. She'd been completely focused on whining about Nat.

Nat....

Maybe this guy worked with him. Maybe he was also undercover with the CIA, and she was just recognizing Nat's coworker from that day at the Tower of London, the day Nat shot the man with the backpack.

No, somehow she knew that wasn't right, either.

She tried to dismiss the nagging feeling. Who cared where or why she'd seen this guy before?

But she just couldn't let it go. Something was wrong, and her instincts were screaming at her to figure it out.

She slid quietly back into a shadow, grateful for the

low lighting in the church, and looked for Megan. Her sister was no more than perhaps ten feet away, enthralled by some stained glass.

Julianna crept over and put her finger to her mouth in the universal *Shh!* sign.

"What's wrong?" Megan whispered.

"There's a janitor over there who I know from somewhere, but I can't remember where. Something's up with him, Meg. Something's not right; I can feel it."

Megan nodded then followed her sister as they silently walked back to where she had been standing before. Megan peeked toward the memorial and looked at the janitor leaning over the bucket, fiddling with something inside it.

He turned his face in their direction, and both sisters froze, fearing he'd spotted them. But he must not have, as he looked back into the bucket again, once more concentrating on it.

What's the fascination with muddy mop water? Julianna wondered. Then she noticed Megan's eyes go wide with fear as she started backing away slowly. Julianna followed her, and when they'd retreated far enough, Megan said, "He's one of the gunmen. From Bath."

"Of course! I knew I'd seen him somewhere—he's Gunman One. What's he doing here?"

"Probably not waxing the floor."

"Oh no! This is it! This is the terrorist activity they've been expecting."

"But what's he *doing?*"

"I don't know, but we need help. And we need to know what's in that bucket," Julianna said. She could feel the panic in her warring with her nurse's instincts to help.

"Why don't you go find Nat?" Megan suggested.

"I'll keep an eye on this guy."

"No, I don't think that'll work," Julianna replied, hoping to let common sense prevail over her need to see Nat again. "If Nat sees me coming, he'll take off in the other direction. He doesn't want to have anything to do with me right now. You go and try to find either Nat or Tom and tell them what we know."

"Okay, you're probably right," Megan agreed. "But don't do anything stupid. He'd probably be able to recognize you pretty easily, you know. You sort of singled yourself out that day."

"Yeah, okay. You be careful, too," Julianna said, giving Megan a quick hug before Megan turned to leave. "Don't forget to look down in the crypt."

Megan nodded and walked quietly toward the back of the church. She stopped to look at statues and paintings as she went, no doubt trying to look like an unconcerned tourist in case the gunman spotted her.

Julianna crept back to where she could see the candle memorial and the gunman, but he was gone. *My detective skills are just amazing....* She'd already lost the suspect, although she doubted she would have followed him very far anyway, even if she'd seen him take off. What would she possibly do if he was fleeing the scene? Perform a citizen's arrest? Hit him with her guidebook?

At least the bucket was still sitting there.

She paused to survey the area, making sure she didn't see his gray jumpsuit anywhere. But she only saw a few other tourists making their way behind the altar. No one seemed to have noticed her, or the bucket for that matter.

She made her way around to the front of the altar, then crept toward the bucket as slowly and quietly as she could. Her nerves seemed to be jangling audibly as she drew closer, but still no one seemed to notice her. And the gunman hadn't reappeared.

One step. *Pause.* Look around. *Pause.* Another step. *Pause.* She agonizingly worked her way to the bucket as fear surged through her veins. But her need to know what was in there and her desire to help kept propelling her forward.

Finally she reached it. She took a deep breath, then leaned over it and looked inside.

The jumpsuit!

He'd stripped it off, so now she didn't know what he was wearing or how to identify him for Nat. Great.

She reached slowly down and touched the fabric, which was still warm from his body. She carefully pulled it aside, then gasped. What she saw then she recognized immediately from her countless hours spent watching more movies than she could remember.

It was a bomb.

Chapter 46

No More Indecision

JULIANNA HAD no idea what to do.

If she was an action-movie hero, maybe she'd cleverly pick the right wire to cut and save the whole town. If she was Superman or one of the X-Men or whatever, she would fling the bomb, bucket and all, into space, also saving the town.

But without superpowers or a script writer and stunt doubles, what should she, a simple nurse from northern New Jersey, do?

She frantically looked around, still wondering if the gunman was lurking nearby, perhaps watching her. She didn't see him, but she couldn't help feeling he was still around somewhere.

Should she scream *FIRE!* at the top of her lungs and get everyone to evacuate? Or try to help Megan find Nat and Tom? *Or should I just stand here and panic, playing twenty questions with myself?*

The whole scenario just seemed surreal. Why here? Why now? She thought about why a terrorist would pick the Canterbury Cathedral. It wasn't exactly packed with tourists today, although how many tourists showed up on any given day wasn't exactly something terrorists could control or predict.

Why here at all? Her thoughts scattered wildly, freezing her in indecision and fear.

Canterbury was synonymous with pilgrimages and martyrdom. For Christians anyway. A place already known for death, martyrs, tourists, and faith. *What better place to strike, really?* she thought. *Sure, why not?*

"Julianna! I found him!" she heard Megan say behind her. Julianna swung around and found her sister and Nat along with several other men and women—Tom included—running down the aisle in her direction.

"Stop!" she said with one hand up. "Megan, it's a bomb!"

"And where'd the guy go?" Nat asked, scanning the altar as they all caught up to her.

"He dumped the gray jumpsuit he was wearing, which I know because it's right here. But I didn't see him do it, so I don't know what he's wearing now or where he went. I'm sorry." *How many times today am I going to apologize to this man?* she wondered to herself.

"But you two are positive it's one of the men from the bus hijacking?" Tom asked.

"Yes," Megan and Julianna answered in unison.

"It's absolutely him," Julianna went on. "It's the guy who let me stay to help the driver."

Tom turned to the group that had followed him in, giving them a description of the man. After they inspected the bomb and had some sort of intense conversation she could only hear snippets of, they agreed to fan out and search for him while evacuating the other visitors.

Nat pulled out a phone and stepped away from the group, probably to call for the bomb squad and backup of some sort, Julianna guessed. Even in the middle of the hectic scene, she couldn't help noticing—and hating the fact—that Nat hadn't looked at her once during the exchange.

Megan approached her and peered into the bucket.

"Wow! How do we know how long until it

detonates?" she asked.

"I don't know. It doesn't have a helpful timer like in the movies," Julianna said. "I've just been frozen, not knowing what to do since I saw it."

"We get out of here, that's what we do," Megan said. "We brought help, and now our job is over."

"Yeah, I know," Julianna agreed before turning her gaze toward Nat. He was standing with his head down, a look of intense concern and concentration on his face. He was definitely "on" right now, completely immersed in his job. He probably didn't even remember she was there. She watched as he ran his fingers through his hair in his trademark *I'm thinking* gesture. Julianna smiled at this.

"Come on, Jules, quit mooning," Megan said, tugging on her arm. "We've got to get out of here. They're evacuating the place now, and Nat can take care of himself. Let's go!"

"Yeah, right behind you," Julianna replied, turning to follow her sister's lead. But a movement up at the altar caught her attention, and she stopped again.

It was him—the gunman. He was creeping out from behind the pulpit, weapon in hand. He didn't seem to notice her, as his attention was completely focused on his target.

Nat! The gun was pointed directly at him.

Still intent on his conversation, he had turned away. The gunman was about to shoot him in the back.

Julianna's world suddenly got very focused. Her earlier indecision melted away, and she knew in that instant exactly what she needed to do.

The man with the gun stood up, steadied his aim, and started firing. But Julianna was already running, her mind intent on making sure those bullets didn't hit the man she loved.

She didn't stop to consider that they might hit *her* instead.

Chapter 47

Fading In and Out

SHE HIT THE GROUND with a thud, her left shoulder taking the brunt of the fall. But it wasn't her left shoulder that seemed to be on fire. It was her lungs. She couldn't breathe without a burning sensation.

Then she realized everything else hurt, too. *What happened? Where's Nat? Has he been hit?*

She couldn't tell right away. Had she succeeded in her self-appointed mission to save him? Why couldn't she focus? Confusion swirled through her mind, but one question managed to remain vividly clear: *Is Nat alive?*

Everything was fuzzy, but she struggled to focus both her eyes and her attention on the face that suddenly appeared above her.

"Nat. Is he okay?" she tried to gasp. She wasn't sure if she was whispering or if the words were even coming out at all. A roaring sound was making her head pound, and her vision was getting dimmer.

"Nat?" she asked again.

She didn't know if the person hovering over her had heard any of it. She struggled to gain control over her body, but the fight for consciousness was just too hard. She finally succumbed and slid into darkness.

*   *   *

She still didn't know what was going on. Why wouldn't anyone answer her? Where was Nat? Was he okay?

"Nat? Nat?" she called. "Please."

She fell back into unconsciousness once more.

A little time passed. A few hours maybe, but it was impossible to tell for sure.

Then—

"Jules, are you waking up?"

She could hear her sister's voice, but it sounded like it was coming from a long distance away. As if Megan was standing at the other end of a tunnel.

"Nat? Okay?" she whispered.

"Yes, Jules, he's fine. You're a hero."

"Is he...here?"

"No, I'm sorry, but he's not here."

Julianna could feel a single tear slide down her cheek, and she stopped struggling against the blackness, letting it claim her again.

I'm dreaming, she thought. She could definitely hear him. Nat *was* there. She tried to force away the enormous weight of the darkness and open her eyes. But she couldn't quite reach the surface. Her eyelids wouldn't follow the simple command to open.

She focused instead on the voice and what it was saying to her.

"Please wake up, sweetheart. I'm here. And I love you."

No, that couldn't be Nat. He hated her.

"It's my fault. I didn't protect you. Please wake up honey. Give me another chance."

Really? Nat forgiving her? Nat wanting a second chance with her? No, she must have died and gone to heaven, because that wasn't ever going to happen in this world.

She slipped away again.

*   *   *

A nurse stood above her now, checking the IV

bag. Julianna blinked a few times, then realized it was dark because it was the middle of the night.

"Hello there," the nurse said cheerfully. "You've decided to join us finally, have you?"

"Nat?" Julianna asked, wondering if he had actually been there. Was he okay? Had she dreamed all of those assurances from Megan that he was fine? Was *she* dead?

"You've been calling for him for days now," the nurse told her.

"Was he here?"

"I don't know, love. Your sister has been here, and I think your parents flew in, too."

"Mmm...thanks," she said, trying not to let her disappointment show. *Did I really think some stupid heroics would send him running to my side?* She didn't regret her actions, but still.... She just wanted him to be alive and safe, even if he wasn't in her life, she reminded herself. And, hey, at least it seemed *she* wasn't dead, either.

She drifted off to sleep yet again.

*   *   *

The next morning, she awoke to find her whole family in the room.

"Hello, darling!" her mother cried, gingerly squeezing her left arm and swooping in for a kiss on the forehead.

"Hey Mom," she replied, smiling. "Where am I?"

"The hospital in London," her dad answered. "So how was the vacation, Indiana Jones?"

"Just terrific. Thinking of moving here," she said with a grimace. Then, turning to Megan, "So what happened?"

"Mom, Dad, can I talk to Jules alone for a minute?" Megan asked. Their parents nodded and cleared out of the room to go find coffee.

"Okay, so what happened?" Julianna repeated as soon as the door closed.

"Well, you apparently leaped in front of several bullets."

"I did? Where was I shot?"

"Where *weren't* you shot? One of your lungs collapsed, one of your ribs shattered, and your right arm's got a hole in it now."

"Wow," Julianna said with a weak smile. "Is that all?"

"Nat tossed me his phone and jacket and told me to try to stop the bleeding and get an ambulance. He took off after the gunman. Eventually the bomb squad, and what might have actually been the entire CIA, showed up, along with an ambulance. They moved you outside, and eventually a helicopter came and took us here."

"So Nat's okay?" Julianna asked. She wasn't going to let this question go until she got a firm answer.

"Yes, but Jules, I haven't seen him since then. Tom called here to check on us the next day. He said they were able to catch the guy and a few of his accomplices. And they defused the bomb, too."

"Oh, well, that's good news then," Julianna said in an obviously weak attempt at trying to disguise her disappointment.

"Jules, when they're done with all their debriefing and paperwork and whatever else they've got to do, Nat will be here, I'm sure," Megan said soothingly. "Tom says they're done with this assignment, so there's nothing to keep Nat from coming."

"He'll need to get my statement," Julianna said, not willing to allow herself to believe that he'd come for any other reason.

"Yes, that's precisely what I meant, you dork," Megan said with a smile. "I'm glad you're okay."

"Thanks, Meg, me too. So, will you ever take another vacation with me?"

"Not if you paid me a million dollars and hired personal bodyguards and escorts," Megan told her with a wink.

Her family eventually left, and Julianna spent the afternoon alternately sleeping and being awakened for various medicines, tests, vital signs, and questions.

It was once again dark outside when Nat finally appeared at her door.

Chapter 48

Change of Heart

"HI," SHE SAID nervously as he approached her bedside.

"You're awake," he replied.

"Good detective work as always, Super Spy," she said, taking refuge in familiar banter before answering seriously. "Yeah, this morning I woke up fully for the first time."

She was suddenly feeling very awkward. She didn't want to leap to the conclusion that he was here to forgive her. He probably just wanted to thank her for thwarting the bombing plot. Maybe he was going to present an official commendation from the CIA or an award or something like that. This speculation that his visit was for business helped her work to beat back the hope that his intentions were more personal. Despite her efforts, though, those hopes were now fluttering wildly in her chest anyway.

"Why'd you do it?" he asked, interrupting these thoughts.

"Do what?"

"Let yourself get shot?"

So much for romantic gestures, she thought dully. "He was pointing his *gun at you,* Nat. He was going to kill you." Her eyes started tearing up.

"I had a bulletproof vest on," he said softly, reaching over to take her left hand in both of his. "What am I going to do with you?"

And so much for the CIA commendation for bravery and plot-thwarting.

"I guess enrolling me in Mensa is pretty much out of the question, huh?" she asked, feeling like a complete idiot now.

"Probably," Nat said, his smile widening.

"I didn't stop to think about it. I just knew I couldn't bear to have anything happen to you. I love you so much," she said, the tears now spilling down her cheeks.

"I know you do."

"But...but you didn't believe me before. In the maze. You said—"

"I said a lot of things that day, Jersey," Nat told her, mercifully cutting off her stammering response. "And I'm so, so sorry for all of them. I was really angry and so completely blown away that you were still alive. I just didn't know what to believe or how to process all those emotions."

"Try not to use the phrase 'blown away' with me right now," she said, smiling. Then she tried to reach for his hands with her right one, but pain shot through the arm and into her chest. She pulled the hand back and squeezed her eyes shut.

"Oh wow, that *hurts.*"

"Then don't try to move," Nat said, his concerned gaze locking with hers for a few moments as she tried to take his advice and relax. It was a little tough, though. His presence, as usual, had her nerves charged and her senses assaulted.

"It's been almost a week since that day," Nat finally went on. "And I've had a lot of time to think about everything that's happened. To think about *us.*"

Julianna continued to lie still, enjoying the feel of

his touch and the look of tender emotions playing across his face, a sight she never thought she'd witness again.

"Once again, I was in the position of thinking you'd died when those shots went off," Nat said. "I turned around and there you were, lying at my feet and covered with blood. Jersey, you've got to quit doing that. I couldn't take it a third time."

"I'm sorry, Nat. I didn't think; I just reacted." She paused here to watch his face, as memories of their short time together raced through her mind. She couldn't believe how much they'd been through in such a ridiculously short amount of time—and how much she loved him. "Hey, wait...you came here before, didn't you?"

"Yes, of course. You didn't think I'd let my human shield rot away in the hospital without me, did you?"

Julianna smiled. "I *heard* you. I remember hearing your voice! You told me you loved me, but I thought I was dreaming. Honestly, I feel like I'm dreaming *now*, too."

"Nope, not a dream. I'm really here, and I'm not going anywhere." He rubbed her hand lightly with his warm, rough fingers. "I read your email, you know."

"I'm really sorry Nat," she said again. She'd say it a million times if she had to, if it helped make him believe it.

"I know, sweetheart. I believe you. I do," he said. "If I didn't before, I certainly had to after everything you did to protect me. I was teasing you before, but I can't believe how much courage you showed. Your bravery and your love, they take my breath away. And the thing is, under normal circumstances I would have gotten down on one knee and begged you to marry me by this point. But that's not what you want, is it? So I don't know *what* to do."

Julianna gasped as her brain wildly processed his words. *He forgives me? He wants to* marry *me?*

He leaned close to her face and kissed her softly on the lips and then on the tip of her nose before looking back into her eyes.

"But more than a proposal, I owe you an apology," he said. "I'm sorry for my role in this too. You were right that I was insisting that you had to do what I wanted without really listening to what *you* wanted. I can see now that you weren't the only one who made mistakes; I played a part in messing up what we had too. So please tell me how we can possibly move forward. Tell me if you can forgive me and how I can make you happy."

The clouds of confusion cleared away, and suddenly she felt no hesitation at all. She finally knew exactly what she wanted.

"*You,* Nat. *You* make me happy. And I changed my mind, by the way. Somewhere in between my alleged death on the plane and my near death in the cathedral, I realized that I do want the same things you want. I want to marry you; I want to buy a home with you and have children with you and adopt cats and dogs with you. I want all those things. *That* will make me happy. I was just too scared to admit it before. I didn't want to risk my heart or my independence. So I just neatly laid the blame on all my poor friends who were getting married. My life wasn't changing like theirs were, so they must be the ones making the mistakes, not me, right? But I was hiding behind my taffeta and tulle phobia. I'm not going to do that anymore."

"So you'll marry me?" Nat asked, happy disbelief

evident on his face.

"Try and stop me," she said just before he leaned down to kiss her again.

"Okay, let's not waste any more time," he said. "Do you want to do it here in London? As soon as you're feeling better?"

"Oh no," she said, shaking her head while sliding a hand into his soft hair. "I've got a lot of people to torture. This wedding's going to be huge...."

Chapter 49

SHE COULDN'T do it—she thought she'd be able to, and she'd dreamed and planned for it. But in the end, Julianna just wasn't able to go through with it.

She absolutely couldn't pick out the ghastliest, poofiest, most ill-fitting, and appallingly expensive dress available, then force all her closest friends to buy one. It just wasn't nice, and she found she couldn't mar the perfection of her wedding day with nasty retribution, as much as she was dying to chirp *And you'll be able to use it again!* at all the victims.

Besides, having a million bridesmaids made a wedding too expensive, and she and Nat were pooling and saving their money to take a big honeymoon and then buy a house. So, in the end, she asked Megan to be her maid of honor and sole attendant. Her sister, of course, accepted immediately and enthusiastically.

"Even if I make you wear a lime green caftan or a hot pink flouncy *Gone with the Wind* dress, complete with hoops?" Julianna asked.

"Even then."

"You're the best sister in the world. You know that, right?"

"Of course," Megan replied.

"Okay, so," Julianna went on, "since you're my best friend and the best sister a person could have, and also since I already tortured you with that trip to London, I want you to wear any dress you want to wear, any color. You go shop for it or pull it out of your closet. I don't care."

"Really?" Megan had asked, looking at her with obvious suspicion. "Did those bullets ricochet off your brain?"

Julianna remembered the conversation with a smile as she stood looking at herself in the full-length mirror. The wedding day had arrived at last, and she was just about done getting ready. Even though white completely washed out her pale skin, she'd gone the traditional route and purchased a flouncy white dress. But it was a flouncy white dress that *she* got to choose, and she felt like a princess in it.

She looked at her hair, which was piled high, flowers peeking out between the curls, all of which was plastered to her head with ten pounds of hairspray. She loved it.

Then she looked down at the flowers she was holding. The bracelet Nat had bought for her all those months ago in Notting Hill dangled from her wrist. She loved that, too.

"Ready?"

Julianna turned around to find Megan standing in the doorway. She looked beautiful in her simple, full-length, sleeveless gown in navy blue. Her short brown hair was curled and drawn back to the side with a tiny silver clip.

"You look fantastic."

"So do you, Jules. Nat's gonna pass out."

They walked together out of the back room of the church, down the hall, and toward their spot at the beginning of the aisle.

"So are you finally going to tell me where this secret honeymoon spot is?" Megan whispered as the organ began to swell with the processional.

"Bath and Stonehenge, of course."

"Get out! Are you insane?"

Julianna smiled. "Where else would we go? It's where we met and fell in love! Plus, we never actually saw anything there."

Megan shook her head in amazement, then turned to make her entrance. Julianna reached for her father's arm and waited for the music to reach their cue.

*   *   *

They walked in together slowly as all the attendees took pictures and smiled at her. She barely noticed any of them because she couldn't take her eyes off Nat waiting for her at the altar. A smile as big as hers was stretched broadly on his face.

It was almost impossible to believe how handsome he was in his tuxedo, and how lucky she was to be walking toward him, ready to join their lives together. After all they'd gone through, it was practically a full-fledged miracle they had gotten to this point. But after surviving that crazy trip from hell and her own long months of rehabilitation, she felt like they could get through anything.

Finally, she reached the front. Her dad kissed her cheek, and then she turned toward Nat, who took her hand. The electricity, which was always present between them, surged again. It never stopped amazing her.

"Hey there, Jersey," he said, "You look absolutely stunning, sweetheart."

"So do you, Super Spy," she whispered back with a smile. "I love you."

"I love you, too."

They smiled at each other, then turned toward the altar, ready to say their vows.

Ready for anything.

Epilogue

"WHAT ARE you *doing* here?!" Nat asked.

"Hi, honey!" Julianna said, surprised to see her husband. She leaned forward for a hug, wrapping her arms around his waist. "What are *you* doing here?"

"Spy stuff. Seriously, what *are* you doing here?" he asked again, looking down at her with concern etched across his face. "I thought you were working today."

"I am," she said, directing Nat's attention to the blood bank's RV used for remote blood donation events. "I volunteered to be the nurse on duty for this mobile blood donation event. They do this every year on the mall, I guess. Didn't I tell you?"

Nat, obviously tense and distracted, was assessing the scene around them as workers set up tables and chairs for the volunteers' use in filling out forms before their donations and drinking juice and eating cookies afterward. He also scanned the mall, from the nearby Lincoln Memorial down toward the Washington Monument. Hundreds of people filled the area, a combination of professionals scurrying to their offices and tourists strapped down with backpacks, cameras, and water bottles.

Soon after their wedding, they had moved to DC. The CIA had reassigned Nat, and Julianna had easily found a new job in one of the capital's many hospitals. Their marriage and move had freed Megan to move closer to her campus, where she was still finishing her degree.

The move was all that had changed for Julianna and Nat. Their love and commitment to each other were as strong as ever, although Julianna had to admit she missed her sister terribly.

"Honey, what's wrong?" Julianna asked, tightening her hold around him.

"You have to get out of here," Nat said, acknowledging her once more. "Go home. Go back to work. Whatever. Just go."

"What? You know I can't do that. I volunteered to be here all day for the blood donations. I can't just leave."

"Listen, you know I can't go into details, but you have to get out of here," Nat said, hugging her tightly in return. "Something may go down here shortly, and I don't want you getting hurt."

"So I should just leave these other workers, all these donors, the hundreds of people who are standing out here, and my husband, and just go home? Watch a soap opera maybe?"

"Okay, sounds good."

"Nat, I was *joking*. And you must be, too. Come on! What's going on?"

"Why are you always so stubborn?" Nat asked, his tone urgent yet gentle. "Why can't you ever just listen to me?"

"Well, if you recall, I would have died in a plane crash if I'd listened to you last time."

"Don't even joke about that! I can't even bear to think about that time during those days I thought you were dead."

"Have I said how sorry I am for that?"

"About a million times. And you're forgiven a million times, too. But please, don't fight me on this anymore. Just cancel the blood drive and get out of here."

"*I'm* the stubborn one? *Me?* When *you* are the one always trying to tell me what to do—" Julianna's tirade was interrupted by a loud commotion.

"He's got a gun!" a woman cried, as screams filled the air. A man standing next to the reflecting pool was waving a gun as people ran away in terror.

"Get down!" Nat cried, tackling Julianna. They landed in the grass, with Nat's body covering hers.

"Are you okay?" he asked, keeping his eyes on the armed man.

Julianna was also transfixed on the scene that was playing itself out several hundred yards from where they lay.

"Yeah, are you?"

"Yep."

Moments later, a swarm of men and women—*must be Nat's coworkers*, Julianna thought—closed in on the man, disarming him without a shot being fired. The crisis was over in a matter of seconds.

"My hero," Julianna said, finally looking back up into Nat's eyes.

"Are you teasing me, Jersey?" he asked, gazing down at her.

"No way, not after that show of heroics."

"Well, it's almost exactly the same thing you did for me in Canterbury," he replied.

Julianna laughed. "Yeah, but I'm not wearing a bulletproof vest."

"Well, you're going to start. Under all those cute scrubs," Nat said, rolling off her and standing up.

"I am not!" Julianna cried, accepting his hand to help her up.

"If you can't stay out of trouble and danger, then you're going to have to at least protect yourself," he said, still holding her hand.

"Seriously honey," Julianna went on, "you've got to stop issuing orders to me."

"I'm sorry; you know I'm not trying to take away your independence or freedom. But if I think your safety is on the line, I'm going to do whatever's necessary to keep you alive. You're just stuck with me and my orders and——"

Julianna reached for him, pulling him into a hug once more and cutting off any further arguments with a kiss.

"Thank you for looking out for me," she said after pulling away. "But just having you in my life is all I ever need."

He leaned back in, kissing her again and tightening their embrace.

She could put up with some occasional bossiness, she decided, because she also knew that right here—in his arms—was exactly where she was meant to be.

Forever.

Thank You!

THANK YOU for reading Julianna and Nat's story! I would appreciate it so much if you took a moment to rate or review it on your favorite site.

This book is part of a trio of books I wrote about women finding and fighting for love on fabulous trips. The first book is *Curveball: A Love Story*, in which Emma travels to Dublin and runs into a sexy American bartender who's in hiding from the mistakes he made and the life he left behind. That story is available in paperback and ebook formats, and it is book one of my Curveball Incident Series.

The second book of this informal trilogy is *The Honeymoon: A Second-Chance Romance*, which is available in paperback and ebook, as well as in Kindle Vella. *The Honeymoon* is about Olivia and John, their catastrophic nightmare of a honeymoon, and the possibility of second chances.

Sneak Peek!

Here's an advance look at my next book, *The Distance Between Us: A Hidden-Identity Romance*. It's the first in a trilogy about three brothers, their explosive family secrets, and their journeys from a shared painful past toward love and acceptance.

This first story concerns Max, who has been hiding from the world since his family's epic meltdown. But his crush on his neighbor, Lily, just might be the push he needs to reach for something more—

CHAPTER ONE

I NOTICED the exact moment it happened, the agonizing instant that the light in her face disappeared behind dark clouds. I knew precisely when it happened because I'm observant like that. Plus…well, okay, it was probably mostly because I've been lurking around and crushing on Lily like a starstruck fanboy ever since she moved into the apartment next to mine almost a year ago. I know all her usual expressions by heart now. Although, to be totally honest, her typical look is whatever expression "bubbly" is, like she was created in a cheerfulness lab and came preset with default factory settings. She's…okay, I know this is corny as all hell, but she's sunshine. Her rays pull me in like nothing I've ever experienced before, because if she's sunshine…I don't know…but I think maybe I'm an eclipse.

It happened immediately for me, that sizzle of

awareness and attraction to her, and I hadn't even seen her gorgeous face yet. I was instantly on high alert from the day she moved in just because of the sound of her sweet voice. I was home working—because, well…I don't really go almost anywhere else—when I heard the banging noises and the grunts and strains of her friends and family as they lifted her furniture and thumped her boxes and knick-knacks into the corners of the small rooms. The walls are thin enough that I knew right away that the new tenant had arrived, but that wasn't what caught my attention. After all, I hadn't exactly been enthralled by the previous tenant, whose name may or may not have been Gus. The most interaction we ever had was me sometimes cautiously waving hello and him occasionally grunting back.

But Lily's moving day? That I noticed. Her infectious happiness can seep right through walls, apparently, because I heard the silver peals of her laughter and the musical lilt of her chatter, and that was it. I was hooked. Because of course she could make even moving into a dumpy apartment sound like eating an ice cream cone on a summer day at a carnival. And, honestly, from that day on, I've been utterly jealous of anyone lucky enough to be on the other side of that wall, able to be on the receiving end of one of those precious smiles.

But even if we weren't neighbors, I still would have noticed her. She's so consistently up, no matter what boring junk she's doing. Checking the mail? She'll laugh and chat with anyone who happens to be in the lobby. Separating out her whites in the laundry room? She's joking with the janitor, who knows her by name—because of course he does—or any of the other tenants who happen to be nearby. She's optimistic, cheerful, and outgoing—basically everything I'm not. I guess that's why I can't get her out of my head. Opposites attract and all that. I'm the weary wanderer dying of thirst in the desert; Lily is the crystal glass of refreshing, ice-cold water, potentially lifesaving but ultimately out of reach.

That's my problem right there. Despite being my neighbor, Lily isn't within my reach. Not for me, good-old, socially shutdown Max. I'm basically locked in a jail of shyness and social anxiety and an inability to speak, and I have been since…always, really, but especially since high school. High school, for me, was like trying to walk in the ocean. You want nothing more than to get your feet under you and find your balance, but meanwhile waves of fear and social condemnation are constantly at work, trying to knock you right down and pull you out to sea.

Acknowledgments

THE BRIDESMAID is the very first book I ever wrote (I completed the first draft more than twenty years ago). You know that stereotypical vision of the English major who just *knows* they have a book inside them? This story was the fruits of that feeling for me.

The first part is a little bit of an autobiography, only in that I was a bridesmaid in a ton of weddings in my twenties, and I accumulated a huge stack of dresses (which I infamously used as U-Haul packing when I moved across the country to New Jersey, lol!). But I'm happy to say that none of my friends were bridezillas, so the comparison ends there!

I wrote this book in the year following the 9/11 terrorist attack (which was also the year I got married). The events of 9/11, as well as a trip I took with a friend to London at that time, were very much in my mind when I wrote this story, and that's largely why I left the story set in the past. The feelings I had at that time play a huge role in the development of this story, and I felt that any attempts to move the story out of that time would change the overall feel of it. Plus, I would have to change the technology, of course, which would make a lot of what happens not make much sense.

I hope you enjoy Julianna and Nat's story. As my first story, it holds such a special place in my heart, and I'd love to hear your thoughts about it on social media or via email!

Thank you to my family and friends for all their support and, of course, to my friend and editor Wil Mara, who's helping me turn dreams into reality.

About the Author

ANNE TROWBRIDGE loves writing romances that hit major emotional beats in swoony, angsty stories in which the couples really earn their happily ever afters. Expect banter, angst, and deeply emotional connections that resonate!

She lives in New Jersey with her husband, two kids, and two dogs. When she's not reading or writing, she's teaching language arts to middle schoolers, which really should involve medals for bravery. She grew up all over the Midwest and somehow still loves to travel and see new places.

Join her and learn more about upcoming books at:

https://www.annetrowbridgebooks.com/

https://linktr.ee/annetrowbridgebooks